a Martian to drop by.

But Brandy knew better than to ignore Aunt Tillie's messages from the great beyond. Even if the messages were obscure.

She eyed her visitor. His elegant jacket was hooked on a finger and slung over a broad shoulder. The smooth cut of his burnished hair and his crisp, tapered shirt and tailored slacks made him look as if he had strayed from the pages of a fashion magazine. He looked like a run-of-the-mill, urbane, sophisticated, successful businessman. If not earthy, at least earthly.

Encouraged, she asked, "May I help you?"

Silvery-green eyes, large and unblinking, locked with hers.

Cat's eyes, Brandy thought, stopping in midstride. Or were they...something more?

No, she told herself stoutly, there was nothing—repeat, nothing—unusual in a man having such wicked, knowing eyes.

Dear Reader,

The festive season is often so hectic—a whirlwind of social calls, last-minute shopping, wrapping, baking, tree decorating and finding that perfect hiding place for the children's gifts! But it's also a time to pause and reflect on the true meaning of the holiday: love, peace and goodwill.

Silhouette Romance novels strive to bring the message of love all year round. Not just the special love between a man and woman, but the love for children, family and the community, in stories that capture the laughter, the tears and, *always,* the happy-ever-afters of romance.

I hope you enjoy this month's wonderful love stories—including our WRITTEN IN THE STARS selection, *Arc of the Arrow* by Rita Rainville. And in months to come, watch for Silhouette Romance titles by your all-time favorites, including Diana Palmer, Brittany Young and Annette Broadrick.

The authors and editors of Silhouette Romance books wish you and your loved ones the very best of the holiday season . . . and don't forget to hang the mistletoe!

Sincerely,

Valerie Susan Hayward
Senior Editor

RITA RAINVILLE

Arc of
the Arrow

Silhouette Romance

Published by Silhouette Books New York

America's Publisher of Contemporary Romance

To Leslie Wainger, a perspicacious editor
who encourages the antics of Aunt Tillie,
Uncle Walter and the Romero Brothers

SILHOUETTE BOOKS
300 E. 42nd St., New York, N.Y. 10017

ARC OF THE ARROW

Copyright © 1991 by Rita Rainville

MORE ABOUT THE SAGITTARIUS MAN
Copyright © 1991 by Harlequin Enterprises B.V.

The publisher acknowledges Lydia Lee's contribution to
the afterword contained in this book.

ISBN: 0-373-08832-9

First Silhouette Books printing December 1991

Printed in the U.S.A.

Books by Rita Rainville

Silhouette Romance

Challenge the Devil #313
McCade's Woman #346
*Lady Moonlight #370
Written on the Wind #400
*The Perfect Touch #418
The Glorious Quest #448
Family Affair #478
It Takes a Thief #502
Gentle Persuasion #535
Never Love a Cowboy #556
Valley of Rainbows #598
*No Way to Treat a Lady #663
Never on Sundae #706
One Moment of Magic #746
*Arc of the Arrow #832

*Aunt Tillie stories

Silhouette Desire

A Touch of Class #495
Paid in Full #639

Silhouette Books

Silhouette Christmas Stories 1990
"Lights Out!"

RITA RAINVILLE

has been a favorite with romance readers since the publication of her first book, *Challenge the Devil*, in 1984. More recently, she won the Romance Writers of America Golden Medallion Award for *It Takes a Thief*. Rita was also part of the Silhouette Romance Homecoming Celebration as one of the authors featured in the "Month of Continuing Stars," and the Silhouette Romance Diamond Jubilee.

Rita has always been in love with books—especially romances. In fact, because reading has always been such an important part of her life, she has become a literacy volunteer and now teaches reading to those who have yet to discover the pleasure of a good book.

Southern California is home to this prolific and happily married author, who plans to continue writing romances for a long time to come.

A NOTE FROM THE AUTHOR

Dear Reader,

My mother was a Sagittarian.

For years, that meant nothing more to me than the fact that her birthday was on December 3, and the newspaper horoscope column—which, it seemed, had something witty or dire to say about everyone—reserved the section called "Sagittarius" for people who were born around that date.

When I first found a book on astrology and turned to the section that pertained to my mother, what I read didn't surprise me a bit. Sagittarians, I read, were above all, honest. They were also blunt. For blunt, read, "not always tactful." That was my mom. Everyone who knew her realized that you didn't ask her a question unless you were prepared for the unvarnished truth.

So when I was asked to write about a Sagittarian hero, I saw all sorts of possibilities. I hope you enjoy reading about Rafferty—a man who, at times, is too honest for his own good!

Sincerely,

Rita Rainville

Prologue

Brandy Cochran poked at the automatic dial on her desk telephone and waited impatiently for her cousin to answer. Jana would know what to do, she assured herself. And if anyone in the world would under- stand— At the sound of a soft contralto query, she said, "Jana? Thank God you're home!"

"Brandy? What's the matter? You sound upset." Jana's calm voice was low and soothing, perfect for a psychologist who specialized in reducing stress in a stressed-out world.

"Upset? *Upset?* Jana, you've got to do some- thing!"

"About what?"

"Aunt Tillie."

The silence that followed was broken by soft laugh- ter. "Haven't you learned by now that no one does anything about Aunt Tillie? We just go along for the ride."

Brandy closed her eyes and took a deep, lung-filling breath. It didn't help. "Look, I love Aunt Tillie as much as the rest of the family does, but I don't want her turning my life upside down—"

"What's she done now?" Jana's voice was resigned.

"—and making me crazy. She's already turned Kara into a psychic—"

"And found her a husband."

"And got you involved with a lot of tree-swinging, primal-screaming clients—"

"And found me a husband."

"And went to Montana and almost convinced Dave that Uncle Walter—who, I shouldn't have to remind you, went on to his heavenly reward well over a decade ago—was one of the llamas on his ranch—"

"And found him a wife."

Brandy took another deep breath. It helped no more than the last one. "What's she doing, going through her nieces and nephews one by one and trying to drive them crazy?"

"What did she—"

"Up to now," Brandy said broodingly, "I've been safely on the sidelines. While she's concentrated on the rest of you, she's just visited me every so often and told me about her daily chats with Uncle Walter."

"Some would consider that enough." There was affectionate humor in Jana's voice.

"Yeah. Jana, I don't want Uncle Walter—wherever he is and whatever he's doing—concentrating on me."

"That's understandable. In our family, strong men tremble when Aunt Tillie looks at them and begins a sentence with 'Walter wants me to tell you something.'"

"I've seen what happens when he gets into the act. Or when Aunt Tillie *says* he does. She goes into action and all hell breaks loose."

"Calm down, Brandy. What did she *say?*"

"She talked in circles."

"So what else is new? She always does when something's bothering her. But you must have understood some of it, or you wouldn't sound so...so—"

"Upset?"

"Yeah. Come on, give."

Brandy sighed. "You're not going to believe it."

"By now, I believe anything."

"She said that Uncle Walter was very specific."

"Oh-oh. It's bad enough when he's vague."

"He said..."

"Yeah?"

"That I'm going to..."

"Yeah?"

"Become..."

"For heaven's sake, *what?*"

"Emotionally involved with an alien."

There was a beat of silence, then Jana recovered. "Oh. Well, I've heard worse. Uncle Walter coming back as a llama is a lot weirder than that. After all, your shop and condo are both in La Jolla, within

spitting distance of the Mexican border. Actually, when it comes right down to it, you're *surrounded* by aliens. They work in town, and the English class you teach at night is full of them.'' Her voice brightened. ''I wouldn't worry. He can always apply for citizenship.''

''Thank you, cousin dear.'' Brandy's voice was dry. ''If that were the case, I wouldn't worry, either. But Aunt Tillie doesn't mean he's from Mexico or Central America.''

''Oh?'' The word was a soft, cautious sound. ''Where *is* he coming from?''

''Good question. Her celestial communications seemed to break down at that point. She got a little foggy and muttered something about Jupiter. Or Mars.''

''You're going to fall in love with an astronaut?''

Brandy's hand tightened on the receiver. ''No. Not an immigrant, either. Jana, she's talking about a *real* alien. From *outer space.*''

Chapter One

She wasn't a smuggler.

One glance was all it took to tell him that. Just one quick look and R. G. Travers knew. Not that he had had a lot of experience with smugglers, collectively or individually. But he was willing to bet his new high-tech office that they didn't come equipped with laughing blue eyes and a smile that would melt glaciers. Having settled the matter to his satisfaction, R.G. shed his jacket and strolled around the classy basket shop.

Curiosity is a vastly underrated trait.

The thought occurred to R.G. as he picked up a basket with a small, silvery signature medallion and examined it. If he hadn't been curious, he would still be sitting behind his desk evaluating the audit instead of watching a leggy redhead in a yellow sundress carry on an animated conversation with a customer.

If he hadn't been curious, he would have merely jotted a notation on the report that still another company had hired several of their minority employees based on the recommendation of one Brandy Cochran. And he probably wouldn't have wondered how one woman—a woman who owned a flourishing business—knew so many unemployed people. Especially people who came from across a border that was less than twenty miles away.

And if his curiosity hadn't been tinged with an element of cynicism, he wouldn't have thought of *coyotes,* the cold-blooded smugglers who traded in human misery. Or of how easy it would be for her to transport a few *los desdichados,* the wretched ones, to this side of the border. How convenient it would be. The owner of a local business merely buying stock across the border. With a large van. Making frequent trips. Forming an established pattern.

But since he *was* curious—and suspicious enough to ignore his own cardinal rule—he had traded the paperwork for a walk down La Jolla's elegant main drag, barely aware of the ocean breeze that ruffled the petunias and geraniums lining the storefronts. He had followed strolling tourists along the wide walkways past art galleries, boutiques and specialty shoppes until he reached the pristine green and white awning of Canastas.

Brandy Cochran's basket shop.

And with every step he'd taken, he had reminded himself that he was an accountant, not an undercover cop. Doing an audit for the Immigration and Naturalization Service didn't turn him into Dick Tracy. Nor

was it a sound reason to personally involve himself in the situation. If he was smart, he'd go back to the office, finish the report and let the INS come to its own conclusions.

On the other hand, it didn't hurt to check it out. In fact, before he drew Immigration's attention to the possibility of smuggling activity and involved them in a costly investigation, he was obligated to check it out. And then there was the unknown quantity. Brandy Cochran. At the very least, he could drop by her place and sniff around before he turned the dogs loose on her.

Yeah, he was curious. The trait came with the territory, although some people in the business controlled it better than others. Better than he did. Bean counters were logical, pragmatic people who, if they were any good, saw patterns and trends emerge from rows of figures.

And he was very good.

He had seen a pattern, so his idle thought had flared into suspicion and grown stronger with every page he'd turned. It had happened before, but in the past he had been content to deal solely with papers and numbers. This time he wasn't.

And now? Now that he had seen Brandy Cochran?

The pattern was still there, but there had to be another explanation. One that allowed for honest, laughing eyes, a mass of reddish-gold hair and a smile that could light up this beachfront playpen of the rich and famous for a week. A pattern that didn't revolve around *coyotes*.

Across the room, Brandy leaned her forearms on the oak counter and listened to her very enthusiastic, very blond friend, Ruth.

"The Terrys raved about the basket, Brandy! They were really touched. When they called to thank me, they said that I'm—" her eyes widened with blatant false modesty "—a most superior real estate agent."

"And so you are." Brandy reached back and absently secured the clip holding her wavy hair at her nape. "As well as a gracious one."

"I didn't tell them that it was your idea."

"Why should you? It was your money that sent the gift. It doesn't matter who thought of it. The first night in a new home is a great reason to celebrate."

"What did you put in the basket?"

"A primo bottle of white zinfandel, two champagne glasses, a delectable selection of hors d'oeuvres from Danny's, along with some chocolate-dipped strawberries and a few truffles."

"Wonderful! God and the escrow company willing, I'll have a couple more first-nighters toward the end of the month."

Brandy grinned. "Just let me know when. I'm always willing to take your hard-earned money."

She waited until her friend swung out the door before turning to the man standing quietly in the corner, his back to her as he examined a large oval basket hanging from the ceiling. He had sauntered in through the white wrought iron entrance earlier, his eyes widening appreciatively as he took in the vibrant interior of the shop. At least she hoped the look had been one

of appreciation. It was hard to tell; his deeply tanned face didn't give much away.

His glance had skimmed over the white walls, two of which were laden with baskets either hanging from brass hooks or arranged on shelves. Baskets that were overflowing with flowers, some holding wine bottles, some with bright-eyed teddy bears. The other two walls were swarming with exotic stuffed animals who sat cheek to jowl with pots of gourmet teas and coffee, potpourri, gift soaps and a host of other items designed to tempt the tourist trade.

From her vantage point at the counter, Brandy had also noted that he had inspected her as thoroughly as he had the store. Now, while his back was turned, she returned the compliment. He was tall, a good eight or nine inches over her five foot five, and he wasn't dressed like a tourist.

He wasn't green, with an antenna popping out of his thick, tawny hair, either.

She gazed at him, a slight frown narrowing her eyes. It wasn't that she really expected a Martian or a Jupiterian to drop by the store for a visit, but the idea *was* there, and had been since Aunt Tillie's hit-and-run phone conversation three days earlier. It wasn't even that she believed it, Brandy assured herself, but no one in the family—at least those with an ounce of self-preservation—ignored Aunt Tillie when she relayed messages from the great beyond. Or wherever Uncle Walter resided these days. Even if the messages were obscure and invariably incoherent.

Wondering if her spritely aunt and deceased uncle had always had this much trouble communicating, she

eyed her visitor. His elegant gray jacket was hooked on a finger and slung over a broad shoulder. The smooth cut of his burnished hair, as well as his crisp white tapered shirt and dark tailored slacks made him look as if he had strayed from the pages of a fashion magazine. The subtle jonquil tie completed the picture.

When he made a half turn in her direction, running well-shaped fingers along the rim of a basket, nothing about his profile changed the illusion. A thick golden brow arched above a straight nose, firm lips and a chin that was—according to one's definition— assertive or stubborn.

Since Aunt Tillie was the science fiction movie buff in the family, Brandy wasn't sure what the current prototype for a space alien was these days. Whatever it was, there was no way that her visitor could be one. He looked like a normal, average, run-of-the-mill, urbane, sophisticated, successful businessman. If not earthy, at least earthly.

Encouraged, she stepped closer and asked, "May I help you?"

Silvery-green eyes, large and unblinking, locked with hers. As he stared down at her, his pupils expanded, reducing the green to a narrow band.

Cat's eyes, Brandy thought, stopping in mid-stride. Or were they...something more?

No, she told herself stoutly, there was nothing—repeat, nothing—unusual in a man having such wicked, knowing eyes.

She definitely had to get a grip on herself. She couldn't allow a two-minute conversation with someone who talked to llamas and deceased husbands to

unsettle her. At least not so much that she saw aliens behind every potted plant.

Of course, that's exactly what she was doing, she reflected with disgust. In the past three days, she had scrutinized every man who had entered the store. Not just looked at them, *studied* them. Checking for pointed ears like Mr. Spock or some other anomaly, she supposed. It would have helped if she had known what she was looking for. It would help even more if she could ignore the whole thing.

Her customer touched an oblong basket, stopping at the small silver tag. His thumb brushed the surface, tracing the embossed flowing script that spelled out the name of her shop. "I like the medallion."

She blinked at the sound of his voice. It was deep, smooth as sin and almost as tempting. "Thank you. All my baskets have them. It's my trademark."

"I noticed." His gaze settled on her face. "Why did you name the place Canastas?"

Brandy grinned, relaxing. Aliens she didn't know about, but a normal, curious male—however elegant—she could handle. "Don't look for anything profound," she warned lightly. "Canasta means basket in Spanish. I liked the idea and I liked the sound. That's all there was to it."

She watched him mull it over, giving the information far more consideration than it deserved. She had a feeling that he handled most data the same way, with deliberation, finding niches for it, not satisfied until all the bits slid into their proper places, all present and accounted for. His eyes flickered and she almost grinned again. Apparently all the bits were settling to his satisfaction.

He looked around. "Nice shop. How long have you had it?"

"Almost three years." Long enough to finally be well and truly in the black.

Brandy waited. Patience was a virtue she was trying to cultivate. At least with customers. She also read people well enough to know that she wasn't going to make a sale until his curiosity was appeased. So far, he didn't have the look of a man whose life would be blighted if he walked out of her shop empty-handed.

Moving down the aisle, she slid comfortably into her sales pitch. "I started out just selling baskets, then I expanded the stock to include all of this." Her fingers lingered on a can of herbal teas. "This last year I began a customized service. Customers can now order gift baskets for special occasions. Anniversaries, weddings, holidays—"

"First nights in a new home."

She flashed him a smile. "Ah, you heard. That was one of my more brilliant ideas. For an additional fee, I even have them delivered."

"If your last customer's enthusiasm is any indication, you should do well." He gestured at the walls of baskets. "Interesting stock. Some of them look handmade."

Her nod carried a tinge of approval. "You've got a good eye. Some of them are. This one, for example." She handed him a softly sculpted oval one. "The man who does this is a genius. I buy everything he'll sell me."

He nodded. ''I don't blame you. Where'd you find him?''

''Across the border.'' She tilted her head in a southerly direction. ''Originally, that is. He lives around here now. So does my silversmith.''

''He came from Mexico, too?''

''Uh-huh.'' Using principles of salesmanship that were so ingrained they were second nature, Brandy took the basket and handed him another, pointing out the nubby weave. After several years in the business, she no longer had to remind herself to keep the customer touching the merchandise, keep him talking.

''A couple of years ago, on one of my trips to Tijuana, I had the most fantastic luck.''

''Oh?'' R.G. hefted the basket.

''I wandered down one of the side streets and discovered a small colony of craftsmen. They were making some of the most gorgeous stuff I'd ever seen. I worked out a deal with them right on the spot.''

R.G. touched the small silver tag. ''Wasn't it inconvenient going down there all the time?''

''It wasn't a bad drive,'' Brandy said with a small shrug. ''I only did it every two or three weeks. Besides, for merchandise like this, I would have driven to Central America if I'd had to.'' Encouraged by his interest, she added, ''Now I have the best of both worlds.''

''Oh?''

''Uh-huh. About a year ago, they all moved up here. I still get all of their stuff, and it's practically at my doorstep.''

''Convenient.''

She nodded. "You bet it is. Not everyone's so lucky."

When R.G. took the next basket, he verified his first impression. There was no ring on her finger. Nor was there a pale line or indentation where one had been. That made it easier. For both of them.

Because now that he had seen her, he planned to do more than take a quick look around and walk away. A lot more. In fact, walking wasn't even on the agenda anymore. Not now. Nor was rushing his report to Immigration. He could sit on it for a few weeks, at least until he could prove the pattern was misleading. He couldn't ignore it, because if smuggling had occurred to him, it was a foregone conclusion that someone at INS would latch on to the same idea.

R.G. tilted his head, mutely encouraging Brandy to continue her story. She tugged at the basket in his hand and handed him another one.

"So, now, practically the whole family is here, and they're all artistic. One makes luscious lace, another tools leather. If you could see the—"

It was hard to concentrate with her blue eyes sparkling up at him, inviting him to share her pleasure in fate's mutually beneficial arrangement.

Sheer luck? He doubted it.

A coincidence? That two years ago her artisans were living and working in Mexico, and now they were all here? Unlikely.

He had a feeling that the Department of Immigration and Naturalization took a dim view of such serendipitous events. In his dealings with them, he had found that they had a strong leaning toward papers, preferably stamped and legal ones.

Brandy drew in a deep breath. "You must be sorry you asked. I haven't given you a chance to say anything. Tell me what I can do for you."

R.G. first returned the basket then withdrew a business card from his jacket pocket and offered it to her. "You can give me ten or fifteen minutes of your time."

"R. G. Travers of Travers Accountancy?" Brandy looked up with a puzzled frown. "Sorry, I already have an accountant."

"Good. The last thing I need is more business. I'm bogged down with an audit I'm doing for the government, and I—" The wary expression on Brandy's face stopped him.

"Audit?"

R.G. nodded. "Yes." A few questions, he figured. A few answers. Twenty minutes at the most, assuming that she was willing to explain—to someone who had no legal standing for asking questions—how she had developed such a wide circle of friends who just happened to be unemployed, undocumented aliens. He could add a letter of explanation with his report, and that would settle it. Settle that part of it, anyway. The rest, the part that had to do with R. G. Travers and Brandy Cochran, was just beginning.

"*Audit?*" Her voice rose a couple of notches. "Do you mean to say the IRS has *private* snoops on their payroll now?"

"No. That's not what I'm saying." But she wasn't listening. She wasn't even there anymore. Between one

word and the next, she had spun on her heel and
stalked to the front of the store. He followed, coming
to a halt when she swung to face him, her back to the
arched entrance.

Frowning fiercely, she said, "I don't believe this.
You guys are really the limit. You almost drove me out
of business the first two years I was *in* business. I
could hardly tend to the store because I was so busy
answering your letters."

R.G. sighed. "Not *my* letters."

"Well, I didn't imagine them. Somebody wrote
them. If it wasn't letters, it was form this or schedule
that. It drove me crazy, and I had to double what I was
paying my accountant, just to handle all that stuff."

"I don't work for—"

Brandy scowled up at him, her hands curled into
small fists, planted belligerently on her hips. "I absolutely don't understand the government mentality.
That mess is all cleared up. My taxes are paid. *In advance.* In quarterly chunks. And now they send
someone out for a house call?"

"I'm not—"

"Probably with another form. Right?" On a roll
now, Brandy answered her own question. "Of course
I'm right. You people have a paper fixation. Everything has to be documented, in triplicate. If you want
my opinion—"

He apparently didn't.

His gaze had strayed to the doorway behind her,
which was just fine with Brandy because the last thing
in the world she wanted was the personal attention of
the IRS. But her relief was fleeting, lasting only until

she saw the expression in his green eyes. It was a pe-
culiar blend of disbelief and reluctant fascination. It
was also a look that made the small hairs stand out on
her arms, because it was the look that people invariably got when for the first time they laid eyes on—

''Hello, Brandy dear.''

When it rained, it did indeed pour, Brandy decided, closing her eyes and stifling a whimper. The
cheerful, breathy voice was as distinctive as its owner,
a petite woman with a mass of short silver curls.

Aunt Tillie.

Many words had been used by various people in an
attempt to describe her favorite relative. Fey, spry,
enchanting, childlike, adventurous, hair-raising,
unique, exotic, warm, loving.

And psychic.

All were appropriate.

A splendid sense of fashionable eccentricity was also
a trademark of the older woman. She had a penchant
for bright colors, yards of drifting fabric and high-top
tennies. Wondering what sartorial splendor would
greet her today, Brandy turned around.

Tillie was adorned in blinding chartreuse silk draped
on her small body like a badly fitting sari. It was secured with a shocking pink elastic harness that
stretched around her tiny waist and over her shoulders. Purple sneakers completed the outfit.

Brandy blinked at the electric fusion of colors then
took the few steps that separated them and gave her
aunt a hug. ''Aunt Tillie, how nice.'' It was a feeble
greeting, she admitted silently, but it was the best she

could do. Having the IRS and Tillie in the same room was making her feel claustrophobic.

Tillie turned up her cheek for Brandy's kiss, staring at R.G., her eyes bright with speculation. "Hmm."

"There are no accidents," she informed her niece in a placid voice. "I knew there was a reason I wasn't to come before this."

Brandy caught the look of birdlike interest and the thoughtful note in her aunt's voice and shuddered. She could feel it coming. Doom. Tillie was going to talk about little green men and R. G. Travers was going to think they were both balmy. He'd go back to his office and tell people that since she was waiting for an extraterrestrial to visit, she was more than likely also into creative bookkeeping. And he'd advise them to put a big red flag on her file and keep her under constant surveillance.

"Aunt Tillie—"

"I know," Tillie patted her arm. "I shouldn't have called you the other night. At least, not—"

Brandy brightened. "You've changed your mind?"

"—until I had it clear."

"It's not clear?" There was still hope.

Tillie moved closer to R.G., studying his face.

"Walter's getting cryptic as time goes by," she said vaguely.

Brandy shifted uneasily. If the stories her family told were true, Walter had always been cryptic. Weird. Not much of a talker. A perfect mate for Aunt Tillie, because she could tell what he was thinking. Usually. "Maybe he changed his mind," Brandy said hopefully.

Tillie circled R.G., her silvery brows peaked in concentration as she examined every inch of his athletic frame. "Pictures," she muttered.

R.G. craned his neck, trying to follow the little woman's progress as she moved around him.

"Pictures?" Brandy echoed.

Tillie nodded absently. "Walter's," she said in explanation. "At first, I thought Cupid."

R.G. looked from one woman to the other. "Walter's an artist?" he asked in an interested voice.

"Then I thought William Tell."

Brandy leaned against the counter and watched her aunt survey the IRS snoop. Her feeling of impending doom was growing stronger with each passing second. Tillie was too interested in him.

Please God, Brandy thought piously, not him.

To various family members, it was a known fact that Tillie was infatuated—make that enraptured—with creatures from outer space. If they gave it any thought, they would also agree that she would do everything in her considerable power to forge a romantic link between one of them and someone in her family. Such as a niece. Any niece. And that she would consider the sacrifice of a niece a mere bagatelle if it resulted in securing an alien for the clan. It was also generally agreed that when Tillie set her mind to do something, she somehow usually managed to do it.

Brandy stared at the two of them, watching her aunt tilt her head and peer complacently into silvery-green eyes. It was one thing to speculate about life on other planets, she reflected moodily. Most people had contemplated the idea at various times. It was another matter entirely to buy her aunt's theory of an honest-to-God space alien. Especially one who had an appearance at a La Jolla basket shop on his itinerary. It was even harder to imagine being courted—or seduced—by one. And an extraterrestrial *IRS* agent? The very thought sent shudders up her spine.

"A man shooting an arrow," Tillie explained. "That was the picture Walter sent."

"He's a photographer?" R.G. ventured.

"A man silhouetted against the dark sky. With stars in the background."

R.G. frowned. "Shooting at night?"

"The arrow made a perfect arc through the heavens, first out, then down." Tillie's hand traced an arc in the air. "Down, down, down."

"Ah, a video." R.G. nodded, apparently satisfied.

"And there was fire."

"A flaming arrow?" R.G.'s frown returned. "That could be dangerous in Southern California. Things are too dry out here."

Brandy sent an imploring look to the ceiling.

Tillie kept her unblinking gaze on R.G.. "You can call me Aunt Tillie," she informed him. "Tell me your name."

Inclining his head, he said, "R. G. Travers."

"Who just happens to work for the IRS." Brandy's voice was frosty.

"No." His gaze locked with hers. "I don't."

"You don't?"

"Archie?" Tillie asked, her blue eyes growing wide.

"Then who *do* you work for?"

"I have my own accounting firm. Right now, I'm working on an audit for the INS. Immigration."

"Oh, for heaven's sake!"

"Archie?" Tillie repeated in astonishment, her wondering murmur lost in the rise and fall of their conversation.

"So why did you come to see me?" Brandy asked.

"Just to ask a couple of questions."

Brandy held up her right hand as if taking a pledge. "I'm a citizen," she assured him.

Tillie's lips parted in surprise and her blue eyes brightened with excitement. "That's it! Clever Walter." Slowly, tentatively, she extended her hand to touch R.G.'s arm, tilting her head in concentration. The small smile that slowly curved her lips was one of intense satisfaction.

Keeping a proprietary hand on R.G.'s arm, she turned to Brandy. "Walter was right."

Brandy broke off in mid-spate, the muscles in her stomach tightening. "How do you know?" She immediately regretted the question. She didn't want to know. She didn't like the look of blazing excitement on her aunt's face. What she liked even less was the sight of Tillie's possessive hand on R.G.'s arm.

Tillie nodded. "It wasn't Cupid I was supposed to find."

"I don't suppose it was William Tell, either," Brandy said, somehow reluctant to give up on the apple shooter.

Tillie slanted a triumphant glance at the tall man beside her. "No." She practically fizzed with excitement. "It was an *archer!*"

Chapter Two

A few minutes later, Brandy stuck her head in the door of the stockroom. It was small, with boxes stacked neatly along one wall, leaving space for a large worktable near the center. It was occupied by her best friend and one-half of her staff. The other half was Darlene, a ferociously efficient college student. "Kit, can you take over in front for a while?"

A plump brunette in her mid-thirties looked up from the box she was unpacking with a good-natured smile and gave a quick nod. "Be right there. Just let me check these teapots off the packing list. Did I hear your aunt out in front?"

"Uh-huh."

"What's Uncle Walter up to these days?"

"Don't ask."

Kit grinned, initialed the paper and took off her smock. "Okay, I'm ready."

When Brandy closed the door of the small office behind her, Tillie looked up from the comfortable little chair she had appropriated. "Why did you send Archer away?"

Brandy dropped into the chair behind the desk, opposite the one in which her aunt sat, not even bothering to ask how she knew. She *knew* how she knew. Tillie was a better snoop than the most sophisticated bugging system; it was no challenge at all for her to sit in one room and know what was going on in another. Nor did her psychic antenna seem to be affected by distance. She did just as well from her cozy home in Rancho Santa Fe, tuning in on her family, regardless of where the various members were scattered throughout the world. Literally. Even wherever Uncle Walter happened to be located.

Now, meeting her aunt's expectant gaze, Brandy sighed. "I sent him away because I wanted to talk with you. And his name's not Archer."

Tillie shrugged. "Archie is a name for a boy, not a man. Especially not a man who's—"

"Whoa. Wait a minute." More or less accustomed to her aunt's cerebral leapfrogging, Brandy thought for a second and finally made the same mental bound from his initials to Archie, and then to the archer or spaceman. "His name isn't Archie, either."

Tillie's bright-eyed smile was maddening. "Walter said...well, of course, Walter never really *says*, you understand, he just...*indicates*." She gazed at Brandy hopefully. "Do you see?"

"No."

"In time, you will."

God forbid. Brandy closed her eyes in silent supplication. She didn't *ever* want to share that particular gift.

"Walter's never wrong," Tillie stated, then stared thoughtfully past Brandy's shoulder. "Well, hardly ever. No, your friend is Archer."

Because Walter says. So be it. Amen. Brandy dug in her pocket. "Look, I've got his business card here. You can see that his name isn't—"

"Otherwise, why would I have stopped spraying my roses?"

Brandy froze with her arm extended, elbow resting on the desk, the card in her hand. "Stopped spraying your—"

"Roses," Tillie prompted gently. "For thrips."

"Thrips?"

Her aunt nodded, frowning at some dark, inward vision. "If you don't get them off, they suck out the juice. Like vampires."

Brandy dropped her forehead against her arm. It had happened again. They were less than thirty seconds into a conversation, and she was completely, totally and absolutely lost. She hadn't the foggiest idea what they were talking about.

"I was on the third bush when he told me to stop."

Lifting her head, Brandy said warily, "Who told you?"

Tillie's silver brows rose. "Walter." The "of course" was unstated, but it was there.

Brandy closed her eyes. Walter. Naturally. Who else joined Tillie in a plot to drive the younger generation of the family to fits of paranoia? She gave a martyred sigh, then, feeling like a straight man, she said, "I'll bite. Why did he tell you to stop?"

"So I could get down here to meet Archer."

"Aunt Tillie, look at this." She waggled the card. "Please. Look at his name. It has nothing to do with a bow or an arrow or an archer."

Tillie gave the card a cursory glance and returned it. Giving her niece's hand a pat, she said, "It's concealed very cleverly. Just what I would expect. They have a very high level of intelligence, you know."

"They?" She crossed her fingers and hoped she wouldn't hear what she was almost certain she was going to hear.

"Extraterrestrials."

Her aunt's pretty face was flushed with excitement, her eyes a dazzling blue. Anticipation charged the air around them. Brandy groaned. Feeling like she was taking aim at Tinker Bell, she shook her head, spacing her words for emphasis. "I don't believe in people from outer space, Aunt Tillie. I don't believe they exist. And if by chance they do, I just don't think visiting my shop would be high on their list of priorities."

Tillie patted her hand again. "Did you believe in thrips thirty seconds ago?"

Brandy blinked. "Well...no. I didn't even know they exis— That was a dirty trick," she added, knowing it wouldn't do a bit of good. Tillie had selective listening down to a fine art.

Tillie nodded. "Exactly. You didn't believe because you didn't know about them." She jumped to her feet and fluffed out her chartreuse skirt. "Ever since Walter told me that someone was coming, I've been doing research. I'll bring you some books.''

''Aunt Tillie?''

The older woman stopped at the door, her hand resting on the knob. When she turned to face her niece, her blue eyes were filled with gentle inquiry. ''Umm?''

Brandy stood up, hesitated, then perched on the corner of the desk. ''Putting all this stuff about spacemen aside—which I don't believe for a minute—why do you think R. G. Travers is the man...'' She paused, searching for a reasonable way to phrase the question. She finally decided that there was none. ''The man Uncle Walter is...talking about?'' she finished rapidly. ''Why not any of the other customers who've been in here the past three days?''

''I told you,'' Tillie said simply. ''I knew today was the day. And when I touched him, he felt...right. He's the one.'' She opened the door, then turned back again, the corners of her mouth quirked in the beginning of a smile. ''Enjoy the Blue Grotto tonight.''

''What?''

''That's where he's taking you to dinner.''

Brandy's eyes widened. ''How did you know he's—'' Her words died away at Tillie's patient look.

The Blue Grotto was not blue.

Brandy allowed the attentive waiter to place an apricot linen napkin in her lap. He did it with a subdued flourish, mutely informing her that he would be dedicating himself to them for the rest of the evening, attending to their needs before they even knew they had them. After scanning the table's snowy table-cloth and gleaming silver with alert dark eyes, he turned to R.G., giving him the same subliminal assurance.

The elegant restaurant had a well-deserved reputation for serving the local movers and shakers. Its widely spaced tables, artfully placed greenery and high-backed rattan peacock chairs offered its clientele an element even more essential to wheeling and dealing than superb food: privacy.

Once the waiter had reverently poured wine into their glasses and taken their orders, Brandy leaned back in her chair and looked at R.G. In the muted light of the small hurricane lamp, his hair gleamed almost gold, his shadowed eyes reflected pinpoints of candlelight. He had a wicked mouth, she decided. It was as beautiful as it was sensual.

"Well," she asked lightly, "what do we tackle first? Your reason for coming to my shop, my reason for hustling you out the door or my delightful, if rather spacey, aunt?"

He raised his glass in a small toasting gesture before taking a swallow of the wine. "Your choice."

"Good. I was hoping you'd be a gentleman. I choose none of the above. Did your parents actually give an innocent little babe two lonely initials to cope with, or are you hiding a deep, dark secret?"

His corners of his mouth quirked. "What do you think?"

"That you have a weird name," she said promptly. "Remus? Rudolph?" She waited in vain for a reaction, then pressed on. "Rochester? I'll get it, don't tell me."

"I won't."

"I know! Rocky."

He shook his head.

"No? Romeo. Reginald? Remington?"

"It's not worth all the effort," he told her. "I inherited two family names. It was a mouthful for a kid, so I opted for initials a long time ago. Now I'm used to them."

"That's it? You're not going to tell me?" She tilted her head and waited. "I might as well share a deep, dark secret of my own. I have the devil's own curiosity, and we're never going to get around to the other things until you tell me. Besides," she added after a moment's thought, "I don't think I can call you by two measly initials. It's too cold. Of course, if you want to settle for 'Hey, you,' or—"

With a sigh, he said, "Rafferty Galen."

"Rafferty." She tried the name several times, testing it, almost tasting it. "It's a crime against nature," she informed him. "Using those initials when you have a perfectly dandy name like—I'm going to call you Rafferty." She narrowed her eyes thoughtfully. "At least for tonight."

"And after tonight?"

She shrugged, her bright hair brushing against her shoulders. "It's a moot point. We may never run into each other again."

They would. They would because he would make damn sure that they did.

R.G. kept his opinion to himself, deciding that she probably wouldn't be too thrilled with it. Brandy Cochran didn't strike him as a woman who was looking for complications in her life. She was worried about something and she didn't have enough of a poker face to hide the fact. Curiosity had diverted her for a minute, but her blue gaze was already gnawing at the problem again.

She was strung as tight as the bow her aunt had been talking about. She had been that way when she'd approached him in the store. Wary. Edgy. Even before she thought he was with the IRS. And later, her eyes had flared with genuine alarm when she'd heard her aunt's voice.

Interesting. Because he had never seen anyone who was less threatening than that tiny woman in the weird clothes. Strange, yes, but not intimidating.

He thought about that while he watched her peer into the crystal goblet to study the straw-colored wine. Even with a worried frown drawing her brows together, she shimmered with...what? Energy? Vitality? Life? Whatever it was, it was sexy as hell.

She was more than pretty but not quite beautiful. At least not with the pencil-thin kind of beauty that models had. The ones who looked as if they had forgotten what a good meal tasted like. On the contrary. Brandy's slim waist was defined by some very enticing curves. Her glorious hair, minus the large tortoiseshell clip at her nape, was brushed back, framing her oval face. No, not a beautiful face. But with its laughing eyes, small, straight nose and generous mouth, it was a perfect face.

She sat there quietly, wearing a pale yellow dress that fell somewhere between prim and seductive, the square neck revealing her tan satiny skin and the vulnerable hollow of her throat. He wanted to vault across the table, toss her over his shoulder and carry her off. To an island. Or the desert. Any place where they wouldn't be disturbed. And she didn't even know. What's more, he decided grimly, she probably wouldn't care if she did know.

Because the lady had a problem.

"About the mix-up this morning," he said abruptly. "I'm not—"

She looked up. "I know. Not with the IRS. Believe me, I'm relieved." Curiosity flickered in her eyes. "So tell me why Immigration is interested in me."

At Brandy's tone of mild inquiry, R.G. leaned back in the chair, his eyes narrowing as he looked at her. He still had a residue of doubt, he realized. A doubt strong enough to tighten the muscles in the back of his neck, strong enough so that the relief he felt at her words was a tangible thing. He believed in her innocence because she was no actress, because her face was too transparent. She had probably never told a convincing lie in her life. Her feelings were recorded in her eyes as clearly as her signature would be on a bill of sale. And now there was no wariness in her clear gaze, no shuttered attempt at concealment. She was simply curious.

"They're not," he told her. "At least not yet. But by the time I finish my report, they may be."

"Why?"

Her bewilderment was as genuine as the curiosity. If he had needed further proof, it was still there in her blue eyes. After the waiter silently slid salads in front of them, he said, "The amnesty program caught the INS understaffed. They hired me to audit a survey of local employers, one that asked them to list the documentation of employees."

Brandy stared at him, her brows knit in thought. "Isn't that discriminatory?"

He shook his head slowly. "Not if the same questions are asked of all employees."

"Oh. Sneaky little devils, aren't they?" She thought about what he had said. "So how did I get into the picture?"

"Your name keeps coming up as the person recommending the undocumented aliens for jobs."

Her look of blank surprise gave way to blazing indignation. "That's it? I'm under suspicion of God knows what because I—" She stopped and scowled at him. "What *would* I be suspected of?"

"Only the possibility," he pointed out.

"Possibility of what, Rafferty?"

R.G. sighed. "Smuggling."

"*What?*"

"Keep your voice down," he said dryly, "or you'll have everyone in here thinking exactly what the INS will think if I turn in the final report without an explanation."

"What's that?"

"That Canastas is a stopping point for some of the local *coyotes.*"

Brandy's lips parted on a protesting sound. When she took a deep breath and closed them, R.G. wished he hadn't warned her to calm down. Brandy in a fury would be something to see, he thought idly. Her copper hair would probably go up in flames.

"You're kidding, right?" She tapped a slim finger aggressively on the tablecloth. "Now tell me the punch line."

"I just did."

"Wait a minute." She leaned forward, scowling at him. "Are you telling me that I may be investigated for smuggling merely because I recommended some people for jobs?"

"A considerable number of them," he reminded her. "Mostly undocumented."

"Of course they are," she said impatiently, "but that's not the point."

"It may be to the INS."

She gave a gusty sigh. "Look, Rafferty, I know the Immigration people have a real problem on their hands. I sympathize with them. But I think they're really reaching with this audit thing. It sounds to me like all they want to do is count people and put them in categories. *I'm* taking people who can't speak the language, people who are sometimes homeless, poor as the proverbial church mice, and finding work for them. Tell me what's so wrong with that."

"Well—"

"Besides, they're usually menial jobs that people around here won't touch."

"If you'll—"

"Even more to the point, it's my job."

"Why?"

"Because it is," she said stubbornly.

"Are you through?"

She nodded, narrowing her eyes at his patient tone. "For now."

"I think the INS would be very interested to know exactly who you work for."

"Who I—" She broke off, her eyes shooting blue fire at him.

"You own a basket shop, right?"

"Right," she snapped. "You know I do. What does that have to do with anything?"

"Just this." He touched his glass, sending a series of iridescent ripples through the pale wine. "If *I* can't see the relation between a shop owner and a stream of aliens, how do you think people who are trained to be suspicious will react?"

"I'll tell you what I think," she snapped, pointing her fork at him. "I think that's the kind of official mentality that puts innocent people behind barbed wire fences. I also think you'd better expand your horizons, consider a few other options."

"Such as?"

"Such as the fact that I have another job. At night. And *that's* how I got into this mess."

"Doing what?" he asked softly.

"You can bet your precious bottom line that it's not leading people across the border! I'm a teacher!"

"A what?" R.G. blinked in surprise, studying her exasperated expression.

"You heard me. I teach. English as a Second Language. I also help my students fill out job applications, and when I'm feeling really subversive, I write them letters of recommendation."

"Who hired you?"

"The city, another group of insurgents."

Diverted, he asked, "How did you get a job like that?"

"By not burning up my high school teaching credentials," Brandy said wryly. "A friend of mine works for the city, scheduling local classes for skills and enrichment. She whined and begged and threw in a bit of groveling until I agreed to do this one." She poked a glistening piece of lettuce with her fork. "I should have known better."

"Why?"

"Do you know why I quit teaching?" she demanded.

He shook his head.

"Two reasons," she said succinctly. "I got tired of dealing with junior thugs who didn't want to learn. But the biggie, the main reason, was forms."

He waited while she impaled a cherry tomato on the end of her fork, certain that she'd have more to say on the subject. A lot more.

He was right.

"There were forms for attendance, for free breakfasts, free lunches, bus tickets and immunizations," she told him, not even trying to hide her frustration. "You name it, there were forms for it. So I handed them out and collected them. Some of them wouldn't come back with signatures, so I'd hand them out and collect them again. That's when I did *my* share of begging and whining. Even resorted to bribery. Anything to get those damned forms back. But you know what?''

The waiter whisked away the salad plates and returned with their dinners. Brandy smiled up at him absently. ''Just when I'd account for every one of those suckers and turn them in, I'd get another batch. Usually government forms. Big, fat, complicated official documents requesting all sorts of weird statistics. If we wanted our federal funding—and we couldn't survive without it—we had to fill them out.''

She broke off a bite of salmon steak and popped it into her mouth. ''When I declared my personal independence and left, I made a solemn vow to myself. If I ever taught again, it would be where the students wanted to learn and the government didn't care a fig whether I taught or not. So when my friend—''

''Whined and groveled?''

She nodded. ''Uh-huh. I agreed to do it. She made it sound like heaven. I would be teaching a friendly, informal class in a park near my house to people who would arrive early and stay late, lapping up information like blotters. And since the lessons are all in English, my less-than-fluent Spanish wouldn't be a problem.''

''So what happened?''

''At the first meeting, my former friend got there before the students and handed me a stack of forms this high.'' Brandy held her hand about six inches above the table. ''Government forms. Something to do with the amnesty program. And since my students can't read or write English, guess who gets to take care of them? I'll be filling in the nasty little bubbles for the next several weeks."

"Bubbles?" He waited again. Patiently. He had no doubt that he was about to learn the connection between bubbles and tedious questionnaires.

"You know what I'm talking about. Those pesky little dots right under directions that say, 'fill in the appropriate circle with a number-two pencil.' They're a pain in the neck." She buttered a bite-size piece of sourdough bread and munched on it. "But that's neither here nor there," she said with a sigh. "I have a habit of telling people far more than they want to know. The trials and tribulations of an ex-high school English teacher aren't very interesting."

She was wrong. He had learned several things, all of them intriguing. For instance, he knew that Brandy had been a dedicated teacher. The regret mirrored in her lovely eyes when she spoke of leaving the profession had been all too clear. And he had a strong hunch that she had been an exceptional one, that along with knowledge her students had been given an abundance of enthusiasm and concern. And loyalty.

He also knew that if you asked her a question you got a verbal set of encyclopedias for an answer. She had no filtering system; she said whatever popped into her head.

"What I want to know," Brandy said, "is how someone like you got in the middle of an Immigration investigation."

He studied her inquisitive expression. "Legally and officially, I'm not. My job is to assess the results of the audit, report my finds, point out possible problem areas and suggest solutions if I have any. Since your name cropped up repeatedly, I got curious. I wanted to talk with you before I made a final report."

He made it all sound so simple, she reflected. So ordinary. "Do you do that often?"

"Get curious?"

"Go out and chase down the answers."

His faint smile answered her. No, he didn't.

"Rarely."

"Then why—"

Brandy broke off when the waiter materialized, cradling a telephone in his capable hands.

"Mr. Travers?" When R.G. nodded, he extended the phone. "Your call."

R.G. shook his head. "I'm not expecting a call."

The waiter cleared his throat. "The lady said you were."

His frown deepening, R.G. asked, "What lady?"

"Your Aunt Tillie."

Chapter Three

"Here." Brandy dropped her key into Rafferty's outstretched hand.

When he opened her front door she stepped around him into the living room and continued the discussion they had begun on the way home. Skirting the fine line between the truth—which would eventually lead to telling him about a psychic aunt and extraterrestrials—and an outright lie, she said, "How could I have told Aunt Tillie we were going to the Blue Grotto? You didn't tell *me* until we got there." It would serve no purpose at all to mention that Tillie had known before *he* had, she rationalized.

"Then how did she know?" R.G. waited, watching her move around the cheerful room. It was a reasonable question. And as questions went, a fairly simple one. So why wasn't he getting an answer? She had evaded it the first two times in the car by giving him a stream of unnecessary directions to her condo.

For a while during dinner, she had lost the wariness she'd had earlier in the shop. Now it was back; it had returned with the arrival of the telephone at the restaurant. R.G.'s thoughtful gaze followed her restless movements, taking in the bright room at the same time. She had been ready when he'd arrived to take her to dinner and hadn't invited him in, so now he took the time to study the background she had created for herself.

She liked yellow.

The pale shade on the walls of the airy condo was a soft backdrop to the more vibrant ocher tones of the floral chairs and couch. The sleek telephone on the corner desk, the bouquet of flowers on the dining room table just beyond the arched doorway and the stained glass Tiffany lamp were all variations on the same theme. It reminded him of sunlight. It suited her.

When Brandy absently touched one of the luxuriant green plants that had taken over most of the room's flat surfaces, R.G. wondered if she talked to them. She probably did, he decided, watching her slim fingers softly caress a leaf. She probably did.

All in all, he mused, Brandy was a very contradictory woman. Her laughing eyes and impetuous speech gave the impression of an independent spirit untouched by the complexities of the world around her. But there was also intelligence in those eyes, and a track record in both the academic and business arenas that couldn't be ignored. He didn't believe for a minute that she had been a failure as a teacher, and she had obviously avoided the quagmire that defeated so many budding entrepreneurs. Her shop was one of the busiest on Prospect Street.

She was obviously a woman of many talents, confident and capable. So why was she so wary with him? And why wouldn't she answer a simple question?

"How did Tillie know where we were?" he repeated patiently.

Brandy perched on the arm of a high-backed chair and eyed him with exasperation. The man just didn't give up, she thought with an inward groan, waving him to a seat on the couch. Persistence, patience and blunt honesty were undoubtedly excellent characteristics for his line of work, but they were a definite handicap in a social situation. His tunnel vision was just as annoying. Once he asked a question he didn't budge until he got an answer. Maddening man. Why couldn't Aunt Tillie have picked on someone with the attention span of a flea? She considered the question with idle interest, a slight smile turning up the corners of her mouth.

"So how did she know?"

Well, damn. He really wasn't going to quit. Shooting him an aggravated glance, she flounced down into the chair. "Sometimes Aunt Tillie has—" she paused delicately "—hunches."

"A *hunch* told her where we were?"

"*Inspired* hunches," she amended hastily.

"Right. She just picked up a telephone book, turned to the restaurant section and randomly selected the Blue Grotto."

While she mentally groped for a better explanation, Brandy sighed and murmured, "She doesn't use telephone books." She saw curiosity stir in his eyes the same instant she heard her own words. "I mean, she—"

"Brandy." He raised his large hand, stopping her. "Why don't you just tell me what's going on?"

Brandy studied the knot of his burgundy tie, stalling. "What do you mean?" Even to her ears the words lacked conviction.

He gave her a level look. "There's something about me or your aunt, or both of us, that makes you edgy. I want to know what's the matter."

"Why?"

"Because it's important."

"Why?"

"That's a whole different discussion. One we can deal with after you answer my question." He studied her mutinous expression and sighed. "Please, Brandy, tell me about Tillie."

"I am *very* fond of my aunt," she finally said. "Understand?"

R.G. understood. If he hadn't, her narrowed eyes would have made it quite clear. She meant that she flat-out adored her aunt and wouldn't tolerate any criticism of that intriguing little lady. Interesting, but not surprising. Brandy was obviously a woman who had strong family ties. And if her expression was any indication, her brand of love came complete with a fierce loyalty and a willingness to take on all comers—a package deal. R.G. also had a strong hunch that if a man was involved, the package would include a passion that would shock the hell out of her.

He meant to find out. Soon.

Brandy cleared her throat, wondering about the sudden gleam of determination in his eyes. "Aunt Tillie has always been—"

R.G. waited.

"—rather remarkable." She paused, thought about the words, then gave a satisfactory nod. "One might even say extraordinary."

"What else might one say she is?" he asked amiably, leaning back and making himself comfortable.

Brandy closed her eyes. When she opened them he was still waiting, watching her with a placid expression. She scowled, not fooled for a minute; Rafferty Galen Travers wasn't nearly as innocuous as he tried to look. No man who had such a prosperous business of his own could be—and with two quick calls that afternoon she had learned that his was very prosperous indeed. No, beneath that imperturbable patience lurked a solid core of determination that would keep him right on that sofa for the next twenty-four hours, or however long it took him to get what he wanted.

Brandy brightened. Well, why not give it to him? Most men found Tillie's gift so unnerving they wasted no time heading for greener, less complicated, pastures. It could be the simplest, fastest way to deal with her aunt's spaceman-archer fixation. With Rafferty gone, Tillie would have to realize that Uncle Walter was not infallible.

With Rafferty gone.

Brandy slanted another look at the big, elegant man sitting so quietly across from her, surprised by her own reluctance to utter the words that would send him on his way. Rafferty was... interesting, she allowed, refusing to acknowledge that her pulse surged rambunctiously whenever he looked at her. Intelligence gleamed in his cat's eyes, and when he wasn't fishing for information, dry humor kicked up the corners of his firm mouth.

Yes, interesting.

And he owned his own firm. That was a plus. Not for financial reasons; Rafferty was a man who would be successful in whatever he chose to do. No, it had more to do with the personality behind the profession. He definitely didn't have the follow-the-letter-of-the-law mentality of a typical civil servant.

Brandy frowned, grateful that she hadn't said the words aloud. They sounded very opinionated and rather snobbish, and that wasn't the case at all. It wasn't even as if she had any violent objections to Uncle Sam's various agencies or agents—other than a deep-seated belief that they interfered far too much in the lives of the average citizen. And that they issued too many forms that they always wanted filled out in triplicate. It was just that she had learned years earlier that she didn't deal well with their fussy efficiency.

But that was all beside the point because Rafferty wasn't involved with them. He wasn't with the IRS, and his association with Immigration was temporary. Once the audit was complete and his famous report done, that was it. Or so he said.

And even if he were more involved, so what? She wasn't leading fugitives over parched hills on dark, starless nights. Or any other kind of nights. She wasn't harboring them in the back room of Canastas. She had nothing to hide.

Nada.

Her involvement with the Latino population revolved around her teaching and her shopping forays. That was it. It was innocent. Simple. Not like some she could mention. Not like—

Oh, God. Aunt Tillie.

Her horrified glance flew to his face again. Was *that* why he was here? Had he heard something? Were all of his questions about her shop camouflaging the real issue—her lively and unconventional aunt? Shaken, she met his green gaze. As usual, his face gave nothing away. He just sat there, waiting.

Waiting for what? she wondered, taking a calming breath and almost choking. For her to drop some damning bit of information about Tillie? Well, he'd wait until hell froze over before that happened.

Her eyes narrowed with determination. If it came to a choice between her aunt and a man she had known for one day, there *was* no choice. Rafferty had to go, and she knew how to speed him on his way. With a few well-chosen words.

"*Now* what's the matter?" Rafferty's voice was calm.

"Nothing!" She cleared her throat. "It's just that Aunt Tillie isn't easy to explain. Or to understand."

His brows rose. "I'll give it my best shot."

That was exactly what she was afraid of. Giving a fatalistic shrug, she began. "My aunt is psychic. She doesn't need phone books because when she picks up a telephone, she just knows what number to call. It doesn't matter who she's calling or where the people are, she *knows*."

R.G. looked startled. "You're kidding."

She shook her head.

He thought about what she had said. "So it's more than a hunch."

"A lot more."

"What else does she do?"

Brandy almost groaned aloud at his fascinated expression. "She knows when we're going on a trip before *we* even know. She talks to animals." *Meddles in our love life.* "She knows if we're in trouble." Giving another small shrug, she added, "All the average, run-of-the-mill psychic stuff you read about."

Rafferty's thoughtful gaze shifted to a spot over her left shoulder. He was quiet, absorbing what she had said. Brandy waited, knowing somehow that when all the bits had settled he would come back, demanding more.

It didn't take long.

"And Walter? Who is he?"

Brandy nodded, satisfaction flickering in her blue eyes. She had expected him to pull in the strands, to make the connections. He hadn't disappointed her. "Her husband," she said briskly. "He died almost fourteen years ago."

"Died? But—"

"Passed on. Went to his reward. Walked through the pearly gates. Whatever you want to call it."

"But she said he—"

"Aunt Tillie refers to it as making his transition."

"—told her that—"

"She talks with him at least once a day, sometimes twice."

R.G. choked. "Talks?"

She nodded. "Uncle Walter seems to be a very articulate soul. My cousin says he talks more now than he did B.T.—before transition. And there's no end to his talents. For instance, he tells Aunt Tillie when to buy and sell stock." She looked at R.G. thoughtfully. "Actually he's quite good at it. She's made a bundle in the last few years. Did you say something?"

He shook his head.

Brandy gave him a brilliant smile. "A couple of years ago he persuaded her to move from La Jolla to a pretty place in Ranch Santa Fe. In his spare time he keeps a sharp eye on all the family members, telling Aunt Tillie when one of us is heading for trouble."

"I don't believe it," R.G. said bluntly.

Brandy rested her head on the cushion behind her and studied his frowning face. He didn't look happy. Good. For a few seconds there, he had looked far too intrigued. "Well," she said generously, "I've had my doubts about it, too. But he *did* warn Aunt Tillie before Kara was kidnapped by bandits in Mexico. And he pointed out the trees with the bodies when Aunt Tillie moved to Rancho Santa Fe."

"Bodies?"

"Of course, I've often wondered if he *really* tells her, or if he's just the scapegoat. If maybe she gets tired of being the bearer of bad tidings and simply finds it easier to let Uncle Walter take the blame. What do you think?''

The sudden gleam in Rafferty's eyes stopped her. He didn't seem stunned or shocked. Or dismayed. If anything, he looked enthralled. She hadn't discouraged him, she realized belatedly. All she had done was whet his interest.

"I don't know *what* to think," he admitted, "but I'll be sure to ask her when I see her."

"See her?" Brandy stiffened.

He nodded. "Monday. That's why she tracked me down at the Blue Grotto. She invited me out to her place for lunch."

"She can't do that!" Not on a weekday. Not when the burgeoning artists' colony—a colony composed entirely of Mexican artisans—had the run of the place.

He eyed her curiously. "Why not?"

"Because she, uh, forgot she was coming in to see me again on Monday," Brandy improvised hastily.

"No problem." He gave a small shrug. "We can make it for Tuesday or Wednesday."

"No!" She softened her tone when his green eyes studied her thoughtfully, taking in every nuance of her alarm. "I think she's...going to be busy the rest of the week."

"There's no rush." R.G.'s gaze lingered on her flustered expression.

No rush. Meaning he wasn't going to give up. Meaning he would simply wait until she ran out of excuses or until her aunt got through to him without her knowledge. Then to satisfy his curiosity about psychics in general and Tillie in particular, he would visit the charming house in Rancho Santa Fe.

Where he would discover a clutch of Mexican artists.

And his mind would turn to papers.

Not just *any* kind of papers. Not sketch pads, not stationery.

Legal papers. The kind required to make that one gigantic, sanctioned step across the border.

Then he would speculate.

And would his speculation end up in his report, making Tillie the focus of Immigration's mobilized forces?

Deciding that she didn't want to find out, Brandy lowered her lashes, hastily reviewing her options. Her effervescent aunt was hell-bent on having a close encounter with her "alien archer," and Rafferty—definitely lower-key but just as determined—would accept her invitation. At this point, Brandy reflected gloomily, the best she could hope for was to tag along and run interference.

She gave him her brightest smile. "Since you've already planned on Monday, why don't we all meet at Maggie's for lunch?"

"The place with all the flowers, overlooking the ocean?" There was a slight upward tilt to his brows but he didn't question the fact that lunch had suddenly become a threesome.

"Uh-huh." Brandy nodded. "You don't look too thrilled," she commented finally. "If you don't like it there, we can go somewhere else."

"I'm sure it's fine, but as long as we're staying in town, how about coming to my new office? It's only a mile from your shop, on Torrey Pines Road. I'll order lunch and we can eat in the conference room." When she hesitated, he added persuasively, "I'd like your opinion on something. And Tillie's, of course."

"On what?" Suspicion laced her voice.

Rafferty got up and strolled to the far end of the room. He gazed through the dark window to the courtyard, frowning at the small amber lights illuminating the meandering walkway and clumps of lush greenery. They should be bigger, he thought, uneasily visualizing Brandy winding her way through the dark, parklike area. Floodlights would be perfect.

He scowled at his reflection in the window. Okay, so it was none of his business. She had managed just fine for twenty-six or twenty-seven years without him. If she didn't worry about the overgrown shrubs and dark shadowed areas, why should he? Until this afternoon she had just been a name, thirteen letters that kept appearing on forms. He had dropped by her shop to take a quick look, he reminded himself with irritation. Not to get involved.

Well he *had* taken a look. A long one. He would still be looking next week, next month. For a long, long time, if he played his cards right. And if he wanted to worry about a jungle that could conceal a platoon of rapists, he would damn well worry!

"Opinion about what?" Brandy repeated.

He turned his brooding gaze on her, blinking at her questioning look. "My office," he said, pulling his thoughts back to the present. "I turned the place over to a decorator, and I'm not sure if the result is too formal. I'd really like to know what you think of it."

Brandy joined him at the window, gazing out at the manicured grounds. It sounded innocent enough, even though she couldn't imagine Rafferty suffering qualms about anything. He struck her as a man who took one look and knew exactly what he wanted. One who then managed in his own quiet way to get whatever he went after. And while his office wasn't exactly neutral territory, it would give Aunt Tillie an opportunity to see him on his own turf and take another good—spell that realistic—look at him. By that time, she thought optimistically, Uncle Walter might have even shed more light on the mysterious alien, might have decided that the visitor had originated on the moon and would be riding an elephant.

"All right." She looked up at him. "How does one o'clock sound? My assistant usually goes to lunch at noon, and I take the second shift."

"Fine." Satisfaction gleamed in his eyes. "Want me to order anything in particular?"

She shook her head. "Surprise us."

"I'll do that." He smiled as he met her quizzical gaze, sensing that she had mentally leapt a hurdle. For some reason she was feeling more comfortable with him, willing to tease him a bit. And whether she knew it or not, to offer a subtle, feminine challenge. He could see the sweet speculation gleaming in her eyes and relaxed for the first time since the waiter had handed him the telephone.

It was going to be all right, he assured himself, studying Brandy's complacent expression. More than all right. He didn't know why she had invited herself along, but whatever the reason, she had just saved him a lot of trouble. When Tillie had told him to bring her niece along with him, he had agreed. He would have brought it up if she hadn't, because he wanted Brandy beside him. Hell, he wanted Brandy. Period. Ever since he'd stepped through the door of her shop.

And now, with tension coiling through his body, he knew he had two choices: say good-night and get out of there, or pull her into his arms, kiss her senseless and watch wariness replace the drift of feminine speculation in her lovely eyes. Common sense and caution told him to move.

"Okay," Brandy said with sudden briskness, turning away from the window, "we'll be at your office the day after tomorrow at one."

"You still have my card?"

She nodded, following him to the door. When he stepped outside and stopped on the tiny porch to look at her, Brandy said politely, "Thank you for the dinner. It was lovely."

"It was my pleasure." Go, he told himself. *Now.*

"Oh, wait."

He halted on the walk, a few steps away from her.

"You never answered my question."

"What question?"

"Earlier, when you wanted to know about Aunt Tillie, you said it was important."

He nodded. "So I did."

"When I asked why, you said we'd talk about it later." She paused, shifting in the lighted doorway when he didn't say anything. "Well," she said impatiently, "it's later. Why was it so important?"

Rafferty rested his hands on his hips, the open edges of his jacket held back by his wrists. Exhaling slowly, he reminded himself that he had tried. Deciding that he was good for about another thirty seconds, he said, "Why don't we talk about it some other time?"

Brandy shook her head. "*Now*, Rafferty," she prodded.

Caution, common sense and all the other civilized trappings of modern man dissipated in an instant, leaving in their place the primitive forces that had driven men since the beginning of time. Astonished by the hunger and possessive demands swirling through his body, R.G. stayed where he was, fighting for a measure of control. Brandy demolished his efforts with one short word.

"Why?"

"Because I want you," he said deliberately. "I wanted you the minute I saw you." He moved nearer with each word, stopping only when the heat of her body reached out to him, when he heard her startled gasp and saw her eyes widen with surprise.

"Rafferty."

He ignored the whispered word. "We belong together, Brandy, and we'll *be* together, just as soon as we get a few things straightened out. We made a good start tonight." He cupped the back of her head with his hand and dropped a hard kiss on her parted lips. "A damn good start."

Brandy stared at his broad back, watching him walk across the courtyard, not even blinking until he disappeared around the end of a building.

Late the next morning, Brandy slammed the door of her red Camero and pointed it toward Interstate 5. A few minutes later she veered east on Lomas Santa Fe Drive and followed one of the winding roads lined with towering eucalyptus trees. As she did each time she traversed the gentle hillside, she thought of the legacy left by the Santa Fe Railroad. Not that altruism had been the railroad's intent when they'd planted three million eucalyptus seeds and seedlings in the early 1900s. On the contrary. They had planned to use the mature trees for railroad ties. When the wood had proven to be unsuitable, the railroad executives had apparently bitten the bullet and walked away from the visible evidence of the error, leaving magnificent groves of trees behind.

She followed the meandering road past sprawling homes and fences draped with acacias, turning into the driveway of Tillie's neat little home. It wasn't actually small, she reflected as she got out of the car and started up the walk bordered by yellow roses. It just looked that way when compared to some of the multileveled mansions in the area.

The house was a sparkling white stucco with a red tile roof. Both it and the blooming garden showed evidence of Tillie's distinctive touch; they were cheerful and blazed with color. The front door was painted an electric turquoise this week. The color changed frequently, apparently an indication of her aunt's moods.

As she passed the ornate wrought iron fence, Brandy peered into the backyard where azaleas displayed their blooms in shaded areas along with other assorted greenery. At the far back, a high stuccoed wall supported the trailing branches of a shocking pink bougainvillea, and a latticed walkway covered with lavender wisteria led to an octagonal gazebo. White and graceful, it was a rose-bedecked Victorian whimsy dropped in the midst of old California.

"Brandy, dear, how nice to see you. Come in." Tillie's greeting drifted out through the screen door before Brandy stepped on the porch.

"You're supposed to keep your doors locked," Brandy scolded gently, stepping inside and bending over to drop a kiss on her aunt's soft cheek.

"Whatever for?" Tillie looked up from where she sat on the floor, her blue eyes bright with inquiry. She was wearing one of her favorite outfits, a purple jumpsuit with a tangerine sash.

"Burglars," Brandy said succinctly, joining her aunt on the floor. "Bad guys. Don't you ever watch TV?"

Tillie's eyes got even brighter. "Science fiction movies. The rest is boring. I know what they're going to say before they say it."

"Well, one thing they say is to keep your doors locked. You just never know who's going to—" Her aunt's patient look stopped her in her tracks. She had forgotten. Tillie had a built-in alarm system. She knew who was coming before they arrived. She'd probably have time to call the police and have them waiting for any burglar dumb enough to select her house for a source of revenue.

"What are you doing?" she asked, hastily changing the subject as she reached for one of the books piled around Tillie.

"Research."

"On what?"

"Archer," Tillie said with relish. "Outer space. Aliens. Extraterrestrials." With each word she thumped a different stack of books with her small hand.

Brandy groaned. "Aunt Tillie—"

"You *have* given it some thought, haven't you?"

"Well," she hedged, "I haven't had much time."

"Then do it now," her aunt said firmly. Clucking her tongue, she added, "We should have had this done before Archer arrived, so we'd be ready."

"How do we get ready for someone from outer space?" Brandy asked dryly.

"You learn about their homeland." Tillie plopped a large book in Brandy's lap and turned to some illustrations in the center. "You learn about landing sites for spacecraft. Look at this."

"*Possible* landing sites," Brandy corrected, studying the pictures. "What on earth *is* it?"

"Pictures of the plain of Nazca in Peru," Tillie said in a gratified voice. "These are lines and pictures on it that can only be seen from the air. Possibly two thousand years old. Some people say these straight lines are runways. And look!" Her voice palpitated with excitement. "A picture of a hummingbird, a figure associated throughout mythology with the arrival of gods." She looked straight into Brandy's eyes. "And what could appear more godlike than people arriving from outer space?"

"Aunt Tillie, you can't really believe—"

"Archer had to come from somewhere, didn't he?" she asked reasonably.

Brandy nodded. "Sure. Probably someplace like Arizona or Colorado. And his name isn't Archer."

Tillie patted her hand and jumped nimbly to her feet. "You study these books and I'll go fix us some lunch. You need to learn something about Archer if you're going to marry him!"

Chapter Four

An hour later, Brandy sat at the table gazing morosely at the food before her. Her head ached and she desperately wanted an aspirin, as well as something decent to eat. So what else was new? she wondered. The same thing happened whenever she visited her aunt around mealtime. The headache came with the territory, and she had learned the hard way that even when Tillie was in top form, her cooking left a lot to be desired. When she was preoccupied, it was abysmal.

Today was obviously not one of her aunt's better days.

Eyeing some slightly dried alfalfa sprouts, a package of individually wrapped bouillon cubes, a small dish of chocolate chips and a jar of mayonnaise, Brandy shuddered. Instead of wasting time wondering what the finished product would have been, she did what any sensible woman would do. She snagged the chocolate chips and popped a handful into her mouth.

What she really wanted was a nice, drippy hamburger, she decided. What she did *not* want was to listen to her aunt say one more word about visiting aliens.

But Tillie had hauled a clutch of books to the table, forgotten about lunch and talked nonstop about her favorite subject. For once, she was making perfect sense—at least as much sense as one could while talking about aliens rubbing elbows with ordinary people. She had shown Brandy countless photos of the arrow-straight lines and stylized animals carved into the Nazca Plain and the mysterious circles appearing in wheat fields in southern England. Momentarily diverted by the circles, Tillie had given a delicate snort and summarily dismissed current scientific speculation about air masses. Her vote, naturally, was for spacecraft shennanigans.

Her blue eyes sparkled while she related the theories of spacemen landing as much as a thousand years earlier and pointed to pictures of ancient rock carvings of what looked like shrunken astronauts. "Some people," Tillie announced with relish, picking up the book of the Nazca Plains and turning to a photo of what looked like random lines, "say that these were definitely landing strips for ancient spacecraft."

Brandy groaned.

Looking up from the picture, Tillie added, "Between what Walter has told me and what I've read, I'm sure that aliens have infiltrated us."

Brandy thought longingly of a cold cloth for her aching head. "Us? Who's us? San Diego County? California?"

Tillie's gesture was all-inclusive. "Everyone! Earth. I think there are thousands of them. Maybe millions. And I haven't met *one*," she said dolefully, sounding deprived. Then she brightened. "Until now. Archer is my first."

"His name isn't Archer." Brandy made the statement automatically, knowing in advance that she would be ignored.

She was.

There was a wealth of satisfaction in Tillie's voice when she added, "Just think, Brandy, when you and Archer have children, they'll be—"

"It boggles the mind," Brandy muttered, not wasting her breath with protests. "Do you have an aspirin?"

Tillie looked around the kitchen as if she expected a bottle to materialize. If one did, Brandy decided numbly, she wouldn't ask questions—she'd simply reach out and grab it. "The bathroom?" Tillie said vaguely.

Brandy found them and took two, thought about an afternoon spent listening to her aunt's convoluted theories, and tucked the small bottle in the pocket of her T-shirt. Returning to the table, she turned the conversation to what she considered a more pressing matter. Spacemen would wait; Immigration wouldn't. "Aunt Tillie, can we talk about your artists' colony for a minute?"

The older woman beamed. "Have you seen Basilio's latest painting? It's very good."

"I'm sure it is," Brandy said hurriedly, stopping her before she got sidetracked. Ebony-haired Basilio was in his mid-thirties and had been her aunt's gardener for two years. Some time ago—it would be a year next month, Brandy realized with a start—he had given Tillie a painting of a field of wildflowers as a birthday present. That had been a turning point in their employer-employee relationship. Upon discovering his undeniable talent, Tillie had become his patron. Possibly his patron saint.

She had turned a barnlike structure at the back of her property over to him so he would have a proper environment in which to paint. To show his gratitude, he had introduced her to his entire family—wife, children, cousins, aunts and uncles—many of whom were artists in their own right. It hadn't taken long for them to join him in the barn. Now there were almost ten of them, Brandy realized, including her basket weaver, her silversmith, and Mega, who did beautiful needlework. All of them were part of the extended family who arrived each morning in a rattling, decrepit pickup truck, calling out cheerful greetings to the neighbors.

That was another thing, she thought, momentarily distracted. In any other affluent neighborhood, the growing colony might have been a problem. Would *definitely* have been a problem. But Aunt Tillie's neighbors doted on her; whatever she did was just fine with them. For some obscure reason, they would cut out their tongues before they'd register a complaint.

Brandy had heard vague references to their devotion from her cousin Jana, who had helped resolve a problem for the neighborhood shortly after Tillie had moved into the house. Sometime, she promised herself, she'd learn the whole story.

Putting the question of his talent aside, Brandy asked bluntly, "Do you know if Basilio is legal?"

Tillie blinked. "I'm sure his mother and father were married. Even if they weren't, it was a long time ago and I don't think—"

"Not legitimate, Aunt Tillie. *Legal.*" When the older woman just gazed at her, a puzzled frown drawing her silvery brows together, Brandy was once again reminded that her aunt lived on a plane where politics and legal restrictions were irrelevant. "Maybe he and the others aren't supposed to be here," she ventured.

"There are no accidents."

Brandy considered the obscure statement that seemed to be one of Tillie's favorites, then tried again. "I mean, maybe he should be living in Mexico."

"*Wherever* we are, it's always by divine appointment," Tillie assured her earnestly.

Brandy felt her headache coming back. "Metaphysically speaking, that may be true, but I don't think you could sell the plan to Immigration."

"We are always exactly where we are meant to be." Tillie nodded, apparently pleased that she had clarified the situation.

"Do you know if they have papers?" Brandy asked wearily, knowing that the question should have occurred to her a long time ago. She should have asked, she supposed. But she wasn't sure, had never decided her responsibility in the matter. It seemed like such a personal question. Intrusive. She had opted to handle the situation the easy way, by keeping the relationship as businesslike as possible. When she gave them purchase orders and checks for merchandise, she simply made certain that her paperwork was accurate. That way she kept her conscience clear and the IRS happy.

"Papers? Yes." Tillie gave a definite nod.

"They *do?*" She blinked in relief. "Are you sure?"

"Uh-huh." Tillie gave another nod that set her silver curls bouncing, then looked longingly at a book with a big-eyed alien on the cover.

"How do you know?"

"Because they collect them," the older woman said absently, opening the book. "My neighbors save theirs and I save mine. They take them to the recycling center."

"Not *newspapers,* Aunt Tillie. Documents. Green cards or whatever they call them. Something that says they're in the country legally."

"Mmm."

"You don't understand," Brandy said anxiously, looking at her aunt's serene face. "This is important. R. G. Travers is doing an audit for Immigration."

"Didn't I tell you they were clever?" Tillie beamed at her niece, absently turning a page. "No one would expect him to be doing that. It's a perfect...what do they call it on the detective shows?"

"Cover?"

Tillie nodded vigorously. "Cover." She repeated the word with an inordinate amount of satisfaction.

"Imagine, an alien pretending to investigate other aliens."

"I don't think that's what it is," Brandy objected. "And I don't think he's pretending. What I *do* think is that he's very good at what he does. And right now, what he's doing is concentrating on the Mexican population in this area. Especially those who come in contact with me. And simply because we're related, you could be drawn in to the picture. You probably *will* be drawn in to it."

"That's nice, dear."

Brandy sighed in exasperation. "No it isn't. I can think of several words that are more appropriate, and none of them are nice."

"Mmm."

"Like trouble. Police. Jail. Hoosegow. Pokey." She watched as Tillie continued to turn pages with every indication of total absorption.

"Look at this," Tillie said with sudden animation, sliding the book across the table to Brandy. "UFO sightings! People all over the world have seen them. Some of them say they've—"

Brandy took another handful of chocolate bits and crunched into them.

"—even been on spaceships and seen little men." she jiggled in the chair, gratification radiating from her. "But *none* of them have seen anyone like Archer."

With her jangled nerves soothed by the chocolate, Brandy decided to try another approach. "You're meeting him for lunch on Monday, aren't you?"

Tillie's eyes sparkled. "Even if Walter hadn't suggested it, I would have called him. After all, it's not everyone who has a chance to talk to—"

"About Monday," Brandy interrupted. "Is it all right if..."

"—a real, live alien, to learn about his homeland, to watch what he eats! I'll be at your shop in plenty of time to get to his office by one." Oblivious of Brandy's startled glance, she added, "Maybe the next time he can come to the house."

Next time? So much for hoping that this would be the one and only visit. Brandy frowned, fully aware that she had failed to convince her aunt that they had a potential crisis on their hands. "Aunt Tillie, you won't say anything to Rafferty about Basilio and the others, will you? At least not until we find out whether or not they're here legally."

Tillie patted her hand. "They are exactly where they are supposed to be," she said serenely.

That evening Brandy sat on her sofa, clad in the man's large, pale yellow T-shirt she wore instead of pajamas, holding the telephone receiver in a death grip. "For God's sake, Jana, you're a shrink—tell me how to make her listen to me!"

"You can't," her cousin said simply. "Aunt Tillie might as well be one of those aliens she's so keen about. She lives in the house in Rancho Santa Fe, she putters in her garden, meditates and talks to Uncle Walter out in the gazebo, drives along the roads and visits us, but she actually *exists*—mentally, I mean— somewhere else."

"But—"

"She doesn't read the newspapers, doesn't listen to the news or concern herself with potential wars. Ugliness simply doesn't touch her. She drifts around in a bubble, coming out when she wants to touch base with one of us. She's protected from all of the everyday stuff that we deal with."

Brandy blinked thoughtfully. "Protected by whom?"

Jana's soft, amused chuckle drifted through the earpiece. "Who do you think? Us."

"But, what about—"

"Uncle Walter? Come on, Brandy, he's usually the one who gets her into hot water in the first place! The last time it happened, Uncle Walter told her Dave was going to have a heart attack. She rushed to Montana, turned the ranch on its ear and finally decided that our dear, departed uncle meant that Dave was going to lose his heart to a perfectly wonderful woman."

Brandy laughed softly. "Yeah, I remember. Dave and Jennifer went crazy trying to keep her away from gamblers and llama rustlers."

"She's convinced that Walter takes care of her, but *I* think he just stretches out somewhere on a fluffy cloud and lets us worry about her. Which we do."

"Hmm." Brandy tugged the soft fabric of the shirt down over her thighs. "What would happen if we just..."

"Left her alone? I don't know. I doubt if we'll ever find out, because none of us are capable of doing it. Could you just sit back and let Immigration raid her place and haul her off to jail or wherever they hold people?''

Brandy shuddered. Ever since she had first considered the possibility, the thought had become a nightmare. She had no idea what actually happened to people who thwarted the INS, but she had a very vivid imagination and could picture her dauntless little aunt drooping pathetically behind a barbed wire fence.

''Jana, I don't suppose you'd like to—''

''No.'' Her cousin's soft voice was firm. ''I paid my dues. Now it's your turn.''

''But—''

''All you have to do is convince Aunt Tillie that that man—''

''Rafferty.''

''That Rafferty isn't an alien.''

''I'd have more luck persuading her that Uncle Walter is a figment of her imagination.''

''And convince Rafferty that neither you nor Aunt Tillie are playing fast and loose with immigration laws.''

''Jana—''

''And convince all of your alien friends to work on getting their papers if they don't already have them.''

''Is that all?''

Jana's chuckle sounded heartless. ''That's it. Let me know how it all turns out.''

At the sound of a small but definite click, Brandy slowly lowered the receiver. Staring at it balefully, she said, ''Well, hell.''

* * *

The next afternoon while Brandy locked her car, Tillie trotted ahead into the glass building that housed Rafferty's new office. Her latest creation, a pea green swathe of fabric dotted with gold bangles, floated behind her. Walking into the spacious lobby just seconds after her aunt, Brandy's brows rose when she consulted the hall directory and found that Rafferty occupied the entire top floor. Riding up in the elevator, she was absorbed with her own thoughts and paid scant attention to Tillie's gentle flow of chatter.

The whole top floor?

"Walter always said to look at the walls. They're—"

She supposed she shouldn't be surprised. Everything about Rafferty, from his smooth tawny hair and assured green gaze to his burnished Italian shoes, spoke of success. She had expected to be impressed. But the *whole* top floor?

"—a dead giveaway."

There wasn't a square inch of property in La Jolla that was cheap. Even reasonable. But prime property that overlooked the ocean? Her mind boggled.

"The inner man is revealed by—"

There was an impressive sense of power in Rafferty Galen Travers, she reflected, watching the floor numbers light up as the elevator silently whisked them to the top floor. It wasn't only physical strength, although for a man with a sedentary job, there was a surprisingly rugged cast to his broad shoulders and large hands. No, it was far more subtle than that. It was a sense of purpose, of commitment, a stubborn pragmatism that left no doubt in her mind that he would finish any project he undertook.

"—what he puts on his walls."

And that, Brandy decided, worried her far more than Tillie's bizarre idea that he was from outer space. She knew from experience how one carefully documented statement on a report could be misconstrued, isolated and taken out of context, and how much the evaluation of information depended upon the mindset of the receiving party.

What little she knew of Rafferty had already convinced her that his final report to Immigration would be concise, comprehensive, detailed and fair. Unfortunately she would be one of the details, a footnote— if she were lucky—somewhere near the end.

And just as unfortunately, the person reading the report—a uniformed official at Immigration—would probably be conditioned to regard footnotes with suspicion. And that person would probably instruct another uniformed official to investigate the Cochran lead.

Staring moodily at a wall panel bristling with knobs and buttons, mental images of a raid at Canastas—led by muscular men with drawn guns—flitted through Brandy's mind. Right before her eyes baskets were tumbling from the shelves, and the customers who hadn't scrambled out the door were lining up against the walls with their hands in the air.

Something nudged Brandy between the shoulders and she jumped. "What?"

"The door's open," Tillie prompted, stepping nimbly ahead of her.

"Oh." Stepping into the large reception room, her first impression was that a minimalist had been at work.

Barely.

Her next was of oak furniture with creamy cushions, sand-colored carpet and several sleek floral arrangements placed in pale terra-cotta vases. A large desk, untouched by paper, pen or possibly human hands stood in the center of the room holding only a state-of-the-art telephone. A series of framed paintings against the cool turquoise walls supplied the only vibrant color in the room.

"He likes the Southwest decor, doesn't he?" Brandy commented idly.

When no answer was forthcoming, she turned. Tillie had stopped at the first painting and was standing transfixed, her excitement palpable in the silent room. After one swift glance, Brandy joined her. The two women gazed in rapt silence at a stylized hummingbird identical to the one carved in the wilderness of a Peruvian plain.

"Hi." Rafferty's deep voice brought their heads around until two identical blue gazes blinked thoughtfully at his welcoming smile. He joined them, moving with the easy, controlled grace Brandy had noticed in the shop. He touched her shoulder and his green gaze settled on her lips with the impact of a kiss. Her heart was still pounding when he lifted his hand in a small gesture that offered the room for their approval and said, "What do you think of it?"

"It's lovely." Brandy spoke hastily in an attempt to sidetrack her aunt who was staring up at Rafferty, entranced. If Tillie *had* harbored any doubts, she reflected gloomily, they were gone. Walter had said to look at the walls and she had looked. What she had seen were replicas of drawings that were roughly two thousand years old. Drawings that presented more questions than answers to a scientific community that still did not know who put them there, why they were there, or how they had been drawn with such geometric precision.

But Tillie had no such doubts. She knew who put them there.

Aliens.

"Your interior decorator did a wonderful job," Brandy assured him. "It should definitely calm frazzled nerves on April fourteenth."

"The paintings," Tillie murmured, darting a contented look at the others on the long wall. "They're most . . . unusual."

Brandy kept her gaze riveted on Rafferty's pleased expression. She didn't need a second look at the art displayed with such simple elegance. She had absorbed the details the day before, when her aunt had thrust a book on the Nazca lines under her nose and given her a lengthy explanation of the figures discovered on the plain.

Rafferty followed Tillie, standing behind her as she gazed up at a large spider. Brandy recalled that the figure, as well as the others, was composed of a single line that never crossed itself. One theory presented had been that the path was a ritual maze, allowing the Nazcas who walked along the lines to absorb the essence of whatever the drawing represented.

Rafferty touched the dark frame. "Glad you like them," he said simply. "They remind me of home."

Tillie's indrawn breath was an ecstatic hiss. She shot a triumphant glance at Brandy. *See?* it said. *What did I tell you?*

Brandy stared at him, aghast. "Home?" she asked weakly, clearing her throat. "Uh... where's that?"

"New Mexico." Rafferty ushered them toward the conference room and threw open the large double doors. The decorator had repeated the color scheme, Brandy noted absently, but added more oak chairs and a massive slate table with a Remington bronze in the center.

"New Mexico?" Brandy repeated clearly for her aunt's benefit. Tillie gave her a patient look.

"Uh-huh." He adjusted the vertical blinds at the windows and turned back to them. "Outside of Gallup, near the Zuni reservation."

"I suppose there's a lot of Indian art in the area," Brandy said helpfully.

"Yeah, it's all over the place." He seated them across from each other and took a chair between them at one end of the long table. "My mother's a potter, so I literally grew up with it."

Tillie's smile was blissful, and supremely satisfied. *Clever,* she mouthed silently to Brandy, giving a jiggle of excitement that set her bangles shimmering. Her sparkling blue eyes said she had expected nothing less. After all, aliens *were* extremely intelligent and would have a perfect explanation for everything they did. An explanation that would divert humans from suspecting their true origin, naturally.

Rafferty removed silver covers from the serving dishes and set them on a nearby cart. "I opted for Mexican food," he said easily. "I hope you like it as much as I do. Careful, the plates are hot."

Brandy received another knowing glance from her aunt, one she was able to interpret as clearly as if she had inherited the dreaded ESP. Mexican food, another clever ruse. Of course he would adapt to the local food, the look said—even if on Mars or Jupiter or wherever he had come from he had existed on bug juice or computer chips. Adapting would be necessary to fool the gullible humans. Even if he hated the stuff, he would have to pretend.

Brandy groaned.

Looking at her with quick concern, Rafferty asked, "Would you rather have something else?"

"No!" She shook her head emphatically. "We love it. The hotter the better." Deftly shifting a *chile relleno* to her plate, Brandy reflected that at least that much was the truth. Which was a relief, considering the tap dancing she was doing these days with half-truths and evasions. It was a comfort to be honest about something. And Tillie, unlike many elderly people, could eat anything. The family had concluded long ago that the atrocities she served as meals had given her the digestive system of a billy goat.

"It's very good, Archer." Tillie swallowed, opened her partially eaten taco shell and lavishly spooned on some hot salsa before taking another bite. "*Very* good."

Rafferty crunched on a tortilla chip, looking down at her, a puzzled frown drawing his brows together. "My name isn't—"

"You're not really worried about the office, are you?" Brandy interrupted breathlessly, choking on a bite of green chili in her haste. "It's perfect."

"He knows," Tillie said placidly. "That's not why we're here."

Rafferty's brows rose.

"The time was right. He knew."

"Knew what?" he asked. After he thought about it, he added, "Who knew?"

"You."

"Walter. But I suppose you told him."

The two women had spoken at once.

"Both of you," Brandy clarified. Tillie's lips parted, and Brandy handed her a bowl. "Have some rice. A lot of it."

Tillie reached out and patted his hand. "Brandy has never been a believer," she confided. "But I am. You can tell me."

Rafferty smiled at her earnest expression. "About what?"

"Aunt Tillie!"

"Your home."

"My condo?" He shrugged. "They're all pretty much alike."

Tillie tilted her head, waiting. Her smile, Brandy decided grimly, could have lured words from a monk who had taken a vow of silence. She wondered what effect it would have on an ersatz spaceman.

"Your other home," Tillie prompted. "In...where did you say it was?" The anticipation gleaming in her blue eyes, her belief that her gentle inquisition would result in an admission that included a galaxy teeming with exotic creatures was too much. Brandy closed her eyes and buried her face in her hands.

"New Mexico," Rafferty reminded her with a slight shrug. "Mountains, sand, clean air, hot days and cold nights. My home town was too small and too quiet. I left to go to college and I've only gone back to visit since then."

"You go back?" Tillie was clearly entranced.

Brandy parted her fingers and peeked out at her aunt. As usual, she was hearing only what she wanted to hear and interpreting the conversation to suit her own notions. Just as often as Rafferty said New Mexico Tillie was hearing Jupiter or Mars.

"How often?" Tillie asked, her shining eyes never leaving his face.

He gave another shrug. "Once or twice a year."

"I've always wanted to see...New Mexico."

"You live near an airport. With the right transportation, it doesn't take long."

Brandy's groan was muffled behind her fingers.

After looking down at her empty plate, Tillie dabbed at her mouth with her napkin. "This has been a lovely party, Archer," she said happily. "Next time, we'll do it at my house."

Brandy dropped her hands. "For dinner," she said hastily. If they made it late enough, Basilio and his crew would be gone. "We'll bring the food."

Nodding, Tillie jumped to her feet. "Sit," she said to Rafferty, waving him back down. "Don't get up, Brandy dear, I'll just run along back to the shop and let you get to know Archer better."

"But—"

"Nonsense. I need the walk. And you know what Walter said. If you don't get to know him better, how are you ever going to—"

"Aunt *Tillie*."

She gave Rafferty a proprietary pat on the shoulder. "You and Walter must have some wonderful conversations. He's told me so much about you."

When the door closed softly behind her, Rafferty examined Brandy's resigned expression. "Just what in the sweet hell was that all about?"

Chapter Five

Brandy stared at his burgundy tie, hoping for inspiration. When none came, she looked up and met his gaze, wincing at the amused determination reflected there. "You don't want to know," she assured him.

"Your aunt infers that I've been talking to a dead man, and you think I don't want to know? Think again." He settled back in his chair and folded his arms across his chest, waiting.

Of course he wanted to know, she thought in disgust. Anyone would—even the unimaginative types who liked their information laid out in neat little columns. Even the analytical, pragmatic types like accountants. She stared at his tie again. At this point, she decided, total honesty wasn't even a factor. But since the whole mad affair had gone beyond logic and reason, how harmful could a few little white lies be?

Brandy began slowly, feeling her way. "Aunt Tillie talks to Uncle Walter so much, I think she believes that *everyone* can."

"She said he told her about me," Rafferty pointed out. "Why? What did he have to say?"

"I think those conversations leave a lot open to interpretation."

"How so?" His green eyes were patient.

Brandy wrinkled her nose. "If I've got this straight, they don't have lengthy discussions. She...sort of picks up symbols and has to figure out what they mean. The problem is, she and Uncle Walter seem to be on different wavelengths, because there's usually some misunderstanding." Deciding that *that* had to be the understatement of the century, she rushed on before he could sidetrack her with more troublesome questions. "Remember how she was talking about a man shooting an arrow?"

"Yeah." He waited.

"Well, you just made things more complicated when you introduced yourself."

"*I* did? All I said was that my name was R.G.—"

"Exactly!" she said triumphantly. "And she heard—"

"Wait a minute." He held up his hand to stop her. "She heard—" his eyes narrowed "—Archie?"

Brandy nodded, grinning at his expression. It was a complicated blend of baffled disbelief and fascination.

"And from there she jumped to Archer?"

She nodded again.

"I'll be damned," he said softly, shaking his head.

Brandy remained discreetly silent, grappling with her response to the next inevitable question. It would be nice if she could remain within touching distance of the truth, she mused. Especially since her face gave her away when she strayed very far. But how close could she stay to a tale of extraterrestrials without sounding as weird as ... as Aunt Tillie? Not very close, she decided glumly.

And it wasn't as if she had the rest of the afternoon to wax creative. If the expression on his face was any indication, she had about—

"But what was he telling her about this archer?" Rafferty demanded. "Why was she so excited?"

Two seconds. A liar's life isn't an easy one, Brandy reflected with a stab of self-pity. Not only did she have to come up with a story he'd buy, she had to be convincing while she did it.

"Aunt Tillie is a dedicated matchmaker," she said reluctantly. "She's always trying to marry off her nieces and nephews." Despite the fact that so far she was still being truthful, she dropped her gaze to the fork on her plate. "And she thinks she has an ally in Uncle Walter."

"The archer," he prompted mildly.

"I'm getting to that." Somehow. "She *thinks*," she improvised rapidly, "that Uncle Walter told her he's found my soul mate."

"The archer?" he asked with a small frown.

She nodded, feeling patches of heat in her cheeks.

"Hey, don't be embarrassed." Rafferty's sudden grin startled her. "We all have a few cra—eccentric relatives in the family."

"I think you've overlooked something here," she pointed out delicately.

He blinked, mulling over what she'd said. "I'm the archer?"

She nodded.

"I'm the soul mate?"

Brandy nodded again, watching uneasily as he lounged in his chair, studying her, a slow smile turning up the corners of his incredibly sexy mouth. "I think if we just ignore it," she said hopefully, "it'll go away."

She shifted restlessly, her uneasiness growing. Rafferty didn't appear to be dismayed. On the contrary. His smile was . . . pleased. No, it was more than that. Satisfied. *Extremely* satisfied. And smug? Speculative? She scowled. Whatever the emotion was flickering in his green eyes, she didn't trust it.

With reason, she decided, jumping when he extended his large hand and wrapped it around hers, his thumb deliberately tracing her bare ring finger.

"Soul mates?" he asked gently.

She nodded reluctantly, reflecting that she may have exaggerated a bit, but the connotation of undying love sounded better than Tillie's bald statement of an intergalactic marriage. "That's what she said," she lied.

"Hmm." He eyed her thoughtfully. "I don't know a damn thing about soul mates. Not what they are or how they apply to us."

"It's like . . . being the other half of a person," she offered. "Being perfectly in tune." Warned by the sudden interest in his gaze, Brandy came to an abrupt halt and gave him a brilliant smile. "Well," she said soothingly, "it's not really important, because—"

"Like being lovers?" he asked deliberately. "Like wanting you, knowing that I wanted you the first time I saw you? If that's the case, then she's on the right wavelength."

His grasp tightened fractionally when she tugged at her hand, then he sighed and eased his grip, lacing his fingers through hers. "And if she and the cryptic Walter are picking up some sexy, ethereal vibrations about us, it's fine with me. They're only verifying what I told you in the first place."

"Rafferty!" Brandy jumped up and paced over to the windows. "You're not hearing what I'm saying." She fiddled with the blinds, peering between them to view the sparkling blue expanse of ocean. Keeping her back to him, she took a calming breath and tried to think of something to bring her stress level down. Something peaceful. Something soothing. Something that had nothing to do with being his lover.

"Look." She swung around to face him, determined to be reasonable. "I can understand your interest in Aunt Tillie. She's—"

"My fascination," he murmured, giving her a lazy smile.

"—definitely different," Brandy persevered, narrowing her eyes. He wasn't going to make it easy. But then, when had anything that involved Aunt Tillie ever been easy?

She swatted one of the vertical slats aside. "So go visit her if you want to. Talk with her. Find out what psychics do in their spare time." She bit off the words impatiently. "Just don't pay any attention if she starts talking about us. Ignore whatever she says, and pretty soon she'll forget all about it." If we're lucky.

She walked back, moved the dishes aside and perched on the corner of the table. "It won't be long before Uncle Walter has her haring off in another direction. Trust me," she said persuasively. "We've been through this before."

"We?" He looked at her thoughtfully.

"The family," she explained. "These things never last very long, so all we have to do is be patient. Actually, we don't have to do a thing, and it will just all blow over. What do you think?" Her eyes brightened. "Is it a plan?"

"Yeah, it's a plan, all right." Rafferty eyed her hopeful smile. "A bad one."

She slid off the table and glared down at him. "What do you mean? What's wrong with it?"

"I mean that I don't want it to blow over." He got to his feet with the fluid grace of a large cat. "I mean, I *like* the idea of us being soul mates."

Brandy backed up, stopping when she bumped into the table. "Thirty seconds ago you didn't know what it meant, and now you like the idea? Give me a break."

"I'd like anything that brought us closer together," he admitted.

Brandy blinked, disarmed by his honesty. Almost. She was also unnerved. *He* unnerved her. He was too close, too determined. And deep within his elegant exterior, gleaming from his eyes, was a predatory, prowling male.

Why wasn't he pouring over ledgers or checking some poor soul's tax return? she wondered distractedly, edging sideways to the corner of the table. Why wasn't he acting like a normal, *proper* accountant?

As it was, there was nothing proper about the look in his intent gaze. It told her as bluntly as his words what he wanted.

Her.

Well, she decided, rounding the corner and taking a step backwards, that was just too bad. He couldn't have her. If he wanted reasons, she had a list. A long one. Between a full-time business, a part-time teaching job and keeping an eye on her unpredictable aunt, she had her hands full. When she salvaged some time for herself, she didn't want to spend it dodging a lethal, sexy man.

Rafferty's large hands on her shoulders stopped her retreat. "Don't run away."

"I'm not." Her reply, she reflected, was more automatic than honest. "I'm just—"

His hands tightened fractionally. "Come here."

Brandy stiffened, as alarmed by the purr in his deep voice as she was by the heat radiating from his body. "Rafferty, I don't think this is wise," she said hastily. "Someone might come in. Think of your image."

"There's no one here. Since I was having company, I told my receptionist to take a long lunch." He stepped closer, pinning her between his hard body and the table. Framing her face with his hands, he murmured, "I have to taste those sweet lips, Brandy. I need to hold you."

"Why?"

At her whisper, his gaze left her vulnerable mouth and studied the wary expression in her eyes. "Because when we're together, the sparks we set off could light up a city," he said flatly. "And even if you're as stubborn as a country mule, you're as curious as hell. As curious as I am." He lowered his mouth to hers and murmured against her lips, "Just a kiss, Brandy."

He brushed his mouth against hers gently, allowing her time to resist. When she leaned against him, he muttered an encouraging sound deep in his throat and dropped his hands, tracing her curves and settling on her softly rounded bottom. She sighed against his mouth when he tugged her closer.

Just a kiss? she wondered hazily, sliding her hands up until they met behind his neck. The heat of his body was a sensual invitation, wrapping around her, enticing her nearer. He didn't try to conceal his hunger. His touch, just as the expression in his cat's eyes, was becoming frankly possessive.

When he raised his head and gazed down at her, she made one last attempt to be rational.

"Rafferty," she whispered, "I think—"

"Don't." His lips brushed hers. "Not now." This time his kiss was deliberate, with none of the restraint, none of the cool patience she associated with him. He opened her mouth with his, gently drew her lower lip between his teeth, cherished it, branded it. Branded her. Drank her soft, hungry murmurs, arched beneath the touch of her fingers in his hair.

And when he let her go, steadying her with his large hands on her shoulders, she met his gaze and blinked. She knew by the determined, stubborn, *satisfied* glint in his eyes that he had claimed her. Without leaving a visible mark, with a touch that was both delicate and overwhelmingly erotic, he had claimed her.

And now he believed a major barrier had been overcome. As far as he was concerned, they were a pair, they had a relationship, were well on their way to becoming soul mates. All that from just a kiss? she wondered again.

Just a kiss?

That massive understatement was equivalent to studying a rampaging river and calling it just a flood.

Rafferty leaned his shoulder against the jamb of the open doorway and regarded the scene before him. A glance at the wall clock confirmed that Brandy had been performing for her class without a pause for the fifteen minutes he had been standing there. He wondered how she kept it up for three hours. He was worn out just watching.

Perform was the correct word, he decided judiciously. She used body English to demonstrate the pictures and words printed on individual pieces of cardboard, staging an act worthy of a street mime. She was presently working on a series of verbs used in everyday movements: stand, sit, walk, run, jump. Settling more comfortable in the doorway, he reflected that he had also been right about her teaching ability. She threw herself into the task with unbridled enthusiasm—heart, soul and her unconsciously provocative body.

She wore an electric-blue jumpsuit, a couple of narrow gold chains at her neck and flashes of gold impaled in her ears. Covered from head to toe as she was, she should have looked as prim as a nun. And maybe she would have if the fabric hadn't clung to her sleek little body like a second skin.

All right, he admitted grimly, maybe he was over-reacting. It didn't cling. But it damn well followed every curve she had, fitting snugly over her small, nicely rounded bottom and pert breasts. The sight of it did nothing at all to relieve the tension in his body, even less to diffuse his annoyance.

Rafferty shifted again, swearing silently. It had been years since he'd had to deal with an almost constant state of semiarousal. Since his teens. Now, every time he was with Brandy, every time he thought of her, his body went on red alert.

Taking advantage of the fact that the doorway was partially concealed by a tall, potted fern, Rafferty surveyed the park's facility with an assessing gaze. It was pretty much what he had expected, a large, sparsely furnished multipurpose room filled with dark-eyed, dark-skinned students ranging in age from sixteen to sixty. They had pulled their chairs in a ragged semicircle, leaving Brandy room to pace.

If what he had seen so far was any indication, she had an uphill battle on her hands. They were catching about one in every ten words she uttered. On the other hand, she had their undivided attention and they seemed willing to participate in whatever scheme she cooked up.

Brandy pulled a chair closer and sat down. "Sit," she told them, watching as they exchanged puzzled glances. Rising to her feet, she said, "Stand." She repeated the sequence until several began to nod, then extended her hands and made a lifting motion, urging them to their feet. "Stand," she said again.

Seconds later, she had them moving around the room, chanting the words appropriate to the action. Rafferty watched them bob and jog, sit and jump, staying where he was until they finally straggled out of the room, clutching handouts she had distributed and calling good-night.

"Adiós, señorita."

"Buenas noches, maestra."

"Buenas noches, profesora."

Stepping forward, Rafferty said calmly, "That was quite a performance."

Brandy spun around with a startled gasp, her hand at her throat. "What are you doing creeping around here like Natty Bumppo?" she demanded crossly.

He grinned. "You sound like an English teacher."

"Amazing." Her voice was dry as she perched on the corner of a long table. Didn't the man own a pair of jeans? she wondered, eyeing his charcoal slacks and gleaming loafers. His tie was loosened, the neck of his pale shirt unbuttoned, and his sleeves were rolled up his forearms. Crisp, tawny hair furred his arms. "You didn't answer my question."

"I came to kidnap you."

"What's the ransom?" she asked, idly swinging her feet and frowning down at untidy stacks of paper heaped on the table.

"Your company for dinner."

"Dinner? Rafferty, it's almost nine-thirty." She gave her watch an automatic glance, emphasizing the late hour. "Who eats a meal at this time of night?"

"People who worked through dinner and are starving."

"That plays havoc with your digestive system," Brandy lectured, sliding down and pulling a large box from beneath the table. She began dumping in the papers.

"I have an arrangement with my innards," he told her, wincing as the papers slid across the bottom of the box, forming a frowsy pyramid. "I feed them when I can, and they stay flexible. Your work sheets are getting wrinkled," he pointed out.

She looked down and gave an impatient frown. "You're right." Dropping her tote bag in on top of them, she grabbed the nearest chair and dragged it over to one of the tables. "I always forget to tell them to put the chairs back," she explained, returning for another one.

"I'll do that." He covered her hand with his, stopping her. "You take care of the locks and whatever else you have to do."

She withdrew her hand and moved away to check the windows. "You don't have to—"

"I want to. Besides, I can move them easier and faster."

"And the sooner we're done, the sooner we can leave?" she guessed, closing the first window.

"Right."

"You really are hungry, aren't you?"

"Starved. Where do you want to go?"

"Home," she said decisively, turning around just as he slid the last chair in place. "I've had dinner. If you'll settle for a sandwich or something simple, I'll feed you."

"That's the best offer I've had all day." He picked up the box and tucked it casually under one arm. With the other, he held open the door. "Ready?"

"I sent the report in," Rafferty said abruptly. He touched his mouth with the napkin and placed it on Brandy's glass-topped kitchen table next to his empty plate. Leaning back in the yellow chrome chair, he added, "Thanks, that was wonderful. I owe you a dinner. Anywhere, any time."

Brandy smiled. "That's a lot of gratitude for a salad and a couple of cold, meatloaf sandwiches, but I'll hold you to it. You mean the Immigration report?"

"Yep." He reached back for the coffeepot and when she nodded, filled her cup, then his. "I tied up the loose ends and got it off by messenger today."

"I'm not sure I like being referred to as a loose end."

"A rose by any other name," he murmured, his eyes smiling at her over the rim of his cup. "I attached a letter—"

"You explained that I teach ESL?" she asked anxiously.

"—detailed and boring enough to do the job."

"Boring?" Her voice rose a notch.

"Relax. Government agents expect to be bored by reports. They're highly suspicious if they're not. They won't give you another thought."

"I hope that statement doesn't fall into the 'famous last words' category," she muttered, stacking the few dishes and carrying them to the sink.

"I didn't get where I am by doing sloppy work," he said mildly, nudging her aside and reaching for a sponge. "Where's your soap?"

"You don't have to—"

"You fed me. I'll clean up."

Brandy's brows rose, but she moved over and silently reached for a towel. Several minutes later, she led the way to the living room and waved him to a seat on the sofa as she dropped into the chair. Keeping her voice casual, she asked, "So, now that you've finished the report, is your job with the INS over?"

"Almost."

"I thought you said you tied everything up. What's left?"

His broad shoulders lifted in a slight shrug. "They'll read it and probably give me a call."

"Why?" Stiffening, she said, "You just said—"

"They now have written proof that I've done my job," he explained, half turning to straighten a crooked lamp shade. He eyed it narrowly then looked back at her. "When they read it, they'll call and discuss some minor point just to show me that they've done *theirs*."

"That's silly."

"You're probably right, but more often than not, that's the way it's done." He shrugged. "It's just jumping through a few hoops. We all do it, whatever the job." When she looked at him doubtfully, he held up a hand, stopping her. "You jumped through some when you were teaching and you jump through some now. They may look different and be different sizes, but they're hoops all the same."

Brandy studied his face thoughtfully. He was right—to a certain extent. But she'd bet the farm that hoop jumping was more prevalent in a man's world. Women didn't handle things that way, at least none that she knew. Women weren't into one-upmanship. In fact, she thought, warming to the subject, if a woman called about a report like that, she would be more likely to compliment the sender on a job well done, in hopes of building a good business relationship.

The peculiarities of men made her think of her session earlier that evening. "What did you think of my class?" she asked with sudden curiosity.

Rafferty's gaze shifted from her soft lips to the anticipation gleaming in her blue eyes. There was humor there, too, and a lazy, feminine speculation that made him want to reach out and grab her. What made it even more potent, he reflected wryly, was the fact that she didn't even know it was there.

He had already decided that she was no actress. Here was more proof. And if he played his cards right, that sexy little gleam would stay right where it was—in sparkling eyes that were just part of the magic known as Brandy Cochran.

And it would be only for him.

Life was just one surprise after another, he decided, prudently reaching out to grasp a pillow instead of following his inclination to thrust his hands in her mass of coppery hair. Surprise was an element he normally didn't welcome. He didn't trust it. There was nothing rational about it. But he had taken one look at her that first day in her shop and known that he had found her—the woman he had been waiting for. The one he had known he would find. Eventually.

His first reaction had been one of surprise. Surprise both at his conviction and the immediacy of it. He didn't make a practice of jumping to conclusions—it wasn't a quality that was valued in his line of work. His mode of operation was to thoroughly research a project, gather data, then evaluate it. He had an innate appreciation for logic, evidence and proof. He also had no illusions about himself; he was precise and pragmatic. The persevering type. And probably dull.

His second reaction had been another jolt of surprise. This time because Brandy *was* the one. It didn't take a genius to look around at the jumble of baskets and see that she was warm, impulsive and thrived in an atmosphere of cheerful clutter. Somehow he had assumed that when the time came his woman would share his appreciation of order and reason.

Brandy cleared her throat. "I asked you what you thought of my—"

"Class." He nodded. "I know. I was thinking."

Brandy stiffened. "Take your time," she said coolly.

Life, Rafferty decided glumly, was not only full of surprises, it was one damn obstacle after another. "You're a wonderful teacher," he said with conviction. "You don't need me to tell you that."

"Do I hear a 'but' in there somewhere?" She watched him through narrowed eyes that no longer held a sexy gleam.

Rafferty sighed. Another thing he was—in addition to being pragmatic and dull—was honest. When people asked questions, they got answers. And since he had never learned to tap-dance around the truth, they were usually blunt answers.

"Come on, Rafferty, I'm a big girl. Tell me."

Tossing the pillow aside, he said, "There's nothing wrong with your teaching and you know it, but doesn't the clutter drive you crazy?"

Brandy stared at him. "What clutter?"

"All those papers. The work sheets you had."

"My handouts?"

"The ones you had spread all over the table."

"There were eight of them," she said precisely. "Eight different kinds. Eight stacks."

"And all your students had piles of papers under their chairs. Then they got more from the table and jammed them all together, folding them up and stuffing them in their purses or pockets."

"Wait a minute," she said, astounded. "Let me get this straight. Are you evaluating my teaching skills by how many pieces of paper were floating around the room?"

"No. I'm not." He scowled. "All I'm saying is that you could be a lot more effective, more efficient, if you had things stored in folders or boxes."

"I have a box," she said smugly. "You carried it in for me, remember?"

He winced. "Yeah, and everything's just dumped in there, with your purse squashing what isn't already wrinkled."

"Tote bag."

"Whatever."

"Is there anything else?" she demanded.

"An agenda wouldn't hurt."

"A what?"

"Agenda. That way you wouldn't forget to ask your students to put away the chairs."

Brandy jumped to her feet and stalked over to the window. "I don't believe this," she muttered through clenched teeth.

Rafferty followed her. "I could help you set up a filing system."

"For *what?*"

"Your work sheets."

"Handouts," she snarled. "They're called hand-outs!"

"All you need are some folders. Or if you prefer boxes, I can show you a foolproof system."

"I just bet you can, but I don't want—" The telephone rang, and she broke off to pick it up. "Hello."

"I didn't know they were called handouts, either," Tillie said earnestly.

Brandy's lips twitched. The humor of the ridiculous conversation and her aunt's timely intervention suddenly overcame her irritation. "You've been eavesdropping again, Aunt Tillie."

"Well, yes, it appears that I have." She sounded puzzled. "I didn't mean to, but somehow I seem to be linked with Archer." Tillie paused, apparently trying to fathom the process. "Ah, well, we must be under-standing, dear. He had a lot to learn before he came here, and I think he did quite well to learn account-ing. Although I suppose you could call it poetic jus-tice."

Brandy blinked. "How's that?"

"Think about it. What would an alien of superior intelligence be most likely to do when he came to earth?"

"Beats me."

Tillie's voice had a triumphant ring. "Learn the system that finances our government, then find the loopholes!"

Chapter Six

"Archer!" Tillie's eager gaze slid past her niece and settled on Rafferty's lean face. "Come in." She patted Brandy absently on the shoulder, peering at the small white boxes both of them carried. "Chinese food."

Rafferty's nod was automatic, even though her words were more statement than question. "Brandy said you liked it."

"My tastes are quite catholic," she assured him, tucking her small hand in the crook of his elbow. Wisps of gauzy yellow fabric trailed behind her as they walked. "One might say—" she glanced heavenward, then smiled at him "—universal."

Brandy snorted softly. Universal, indeed. The older woman had never been known for her subtlety, but this was a trifle blatant, even for her. "Come on," she ordered, leading the way to the back of the house.

"Let's get this stuff in the kitchen before it starts dripping."

"Put it in the oven," Tillie directed absently, keeping her hand on Rafferty's arm while he set cartons of food and beer on the tiled counter. "I want to show Archer the yard." Tillie's soft voice drifted back as she led Rafferty out the back door, answering his idle question about the Chinese gong in the dining room. "It's one of my favorite things," she told him.

Brandy stared after them, a wry expression on her face. Remember your role, my girl, she told herself briskly, stacking the boxes on a cookie sheet and sliding them into the oven. At least, your role as Aunt Tillie sees it. You're merely a lure, a brood mare in this little drama. Your job is to snag an alien and produce a batch of fledgling aliens for your favorite auntie. That's all you have to do. The position doesn't require brains or talent. Just the ability to stand still and smile while a predator bears down on you.

Her hands stilled and she wondered anxiously how disappointed Tillie was going to be when this was all over, when the dust had settled and there was no marriage, no alien, no children. After several long moments of reflection, she gave a philosophical shrug. As Tillie had so often remarked, there were no accidents. There must be a reason for this insane situation. She hoped that Tillie truly believed what she preached, because she would need something to sustain her when she learned that her alien was merely a figment of her fertile imagination.

Brandy finished the small task quickly and went outside to find the wanderers. She caught up with them under the flower-framed walkway, stopping just short of where they stood, grinning at the baffled expression on Rafferty's face.

"Wis-te-ri-a," Tillie lectured gently, cupping a cluster of blossoms in her small hands. "There are also varieties in blue, pink and white flowers. Lovely, don't you think? Oh, Brandy." She turned to give her niece an excited smile. "Archer asked about the flowers. I think he wants to learn about the ones we grow here." She looked back up at him. "It's a very clever thing to do, to keep learning, I mean. Most important. After all, the better you understand us, the better you fit in."

Rafferty blinked. "Fit in?"

"You've painted the gazebo," Brandy said hurriedly, pointing to the sparkling white Victorian fancy. It was a feeble effort, she reflected with a sigh, but the best she could come up with on short notice. It was going to be a long evening if Tillie kept tossing out those tantalizing little you-almost-act-like-the-rest-of-us comments.

Tillie cast a fond glance at the airy structure and trotted over to it, waiting until they followed. "Lovely, isn't it? Basilio finished it last week." She urged them up the four shallow stairs with a wave of her hand. "Come sit down and think peaceful thoughts. It settles your nerves."

After arranging drifts of yellow fabric over her knees, she gazed around complacently. "This is where I come to talk with Walter. At least once a day. Sometimes more often. That's where he sits," she added, pointing to the wicker chair Rafferty had just claimed. With a startled apology, he surged to his feet, reluctantly lowering himself again when she waved him back down. "Walter won't mind a bit," she assured him. "You know how generous he is. He'll do anything for a friend."

When Rafferty's hands tightened on the arms of the chair, she gave him a thoughtful look then turned to Brandy. "Very spiky vibrations," she confided. "I think he's a little edgy."

"Damn straight," Rafferty muttered.

Tillie gazed out over the garden, a focused, inward expression on her face. When she turned back to him, her brows were drawn together in a small frown. "Strange. You never...I wouldn't have thought...or have you forgotten how to use it?" she demanded.

"Use what?"

She gazed at him expectantly. "The fast way to discuss things. Mental communication." When he just stared at her, she prodded, "Telepathy."

He shook his head. "Forgotten? Impossible."

"Ah." Tillie settled back with a rapturous look.

"I couldn't forget because I never knew how." He got to his feet. "I think I need a beer. Can I bring you one?"

Both women nodded. "I put them in the refrigerator," Brandy murmured, her gaze absently approving as she watched his lithe, catlike stride cover the distance to the house. He didn't look like a man who spent most of his time behind a desk, she reflected, contemplating his narrow hips and flat stomach. He didn't move like one, either.

It was also obvious that Rafferty didn't share her definition of casual, she decided with a grin. She hadn't convinced him to wear jeans, but at least the suit was gone. Wondering if he ever got rumpled or dirty, she looked down ruefully at the bright yellow shirt that matched her jeans and sneakers. Her style was a definite statement of comfort; his was nothing short of elegance.

Rafferty's white knit shirt stretched over surprisingly broad shoulders and was tucked neatly into the narrow waistband of sharply creased faded denims. The leather running shoes he wore were so white they sparkled. He looked like a model about to shoot a commercial, she reflected with a grin, knowing he would hate the idea. He would be stepping out of a sinfully expensive car, she decided. Or standing on the deck of a yacht wearing one of those watches that cost the earth.

Brandy tucked her knees close to her chest and wrapped her arms around them, pondering. In one of his power suits, Rafferty had all the earmarks of a corporate shark—he was elegant and just a tad dangerous. Today, casual and relaxed, he still managed to look lean and powerful and a touch predatory. He looked...

"Sexy," Tillie offered.

"Hmm?"

"Isn't that the word you were looking for?"

"Don't try that wide-eyed innocence on me, Aunt Tillie. I'm immune."

"Well, he is."

"There's absolutely no privacy in this family," Brandy grumbled. "That was a private conversation." Eyeing her aunt narrowly, she asked, "Why the frown?"

Tillie sighed, her pensive gaze resting on the wisteria-draped walkway. "Archer...puzzles me."

"What's to puzzle?"

"Everything. When I touch him, I *know* that he's the one Walter talked about. The one he said was coming for you."

Brandy's heart jolted. "Then what's the problem?"

"I can't talk with him."

"Can't talk? You two chatter all the time."

"I mean...in other ways."

"Other?" Brandy asked cautiously.

Tillie made a vague gesture with one hand. "We should be able to communicate...."

"Yeah?"

"Without words. The way Walter and I do."

"You mean in your heads?"

"Well, yes." Tillie sighed. "More or less."

"How do you know for sure that he can even do it?"

"Because the books say so. *All* aliens can."

Considering that a comment on the sensational elements of the material that Tillie had used for research would be futile, Brandy said, "Maybe he can only do it with people who come from...wherever he comes from." Like New Mexico.

"But even if he didn't talk to *me,* I should be able to..."

"Tune in?"

Tillie nodded. "Exactly."

''Well, maybe he can put up some sort of a shield. I saw a movie one time about things like that.''

''About extraterrestrials?''

''Probably. It was science fiction.'' One of the few she had ever seen. As far as she could remember, she hadn't bought the premise and had spent an evening memorable only for its boredom.

When Tillie brightened, she winced. If she was a good niece, she wouldn't encourage her aunt in these ridiculous flights of fancy, Brandy told herself. If she was a proper niece, she would persuade her aunt to look at things more realistically.

But where Tillie was concerned, she was neither good nor proper. What she was, was a marshmallow. One look at her aunt's bright face was all it took. She would do a lot—even entertain aliens—before she'd crush her aunt's illusions. If Tillie wanted to talk to Walter, that was just fine with her. If Tillie wanted to believe that Rafferty had arrived via spacecraft rather than birth canal, that was fine, too. ''Let me see if I've got this straight,'' Brandy said. ''Rafferty—''

''Archer.''

''Whatever. That guy in the kitchen is the man Uncle Walter told you about, right? The one that I would meet and marry?''

''Right.''

''You pick up all the right vibes where that's concerned?''

Tillie nodded.

''But you're not picking up the feeling that he's an alien?''

Tillie looked affronted. "I *know* he is. But I can't... I did so want to... when I *do* pick up something, it's just questions about me."

"What's so odd about that?"

"I don't understand why he'd have to wonder. Why he just wouldn't know whatever it is that he wants to know." She blinked thoughtfully. "Maybe he's a very high-level person, specially trained to conceal his abilities. Maybe he's had to train himself to think like us, with all of our restrictions. If he's been on this planet for a long time, he's probably learned a lot of tricks."

"Aunt Tillie," Brandy said carefully, "could it be that you're wrong? That he's not really—"

The older woman shook her head. "I know that he is." She spoke with absolute assurance. "But he's very clever, Brandy. Very intelligent. He doesn't show a trace of any extraordinary traits. That's why he's so clever. Somehow, he's clouded all of his capabilities. I can pry and probe inside his head all I want, and he doesn't give away a thing. He just seems like any mortal—with no more ESP than a hunk of rock!"

Brandy grinned at the other woman's indignant look. "Why don't you ask Uncle Walter to tell you more about him?"

Tillie frowned. "Walter is..."

"Is what?" Gone? Disappeared? Speechless? They should be so lucky.

"Preoccupied," Tillie finally said. A distinct touch of annoyance flavored the word. "He seems very involved with something right now, and isn't paying much attention to me."

"Maybe you should—"

"Shhh! Here he comes!"

"*Walter?*" Brandy looked around in horror.

Waving cheerfully, Tillie called, "Yoo-hoo, Archer! Did you happen to notice the time while you were in the kitchen?"

Brandy settled back, more relieved than she would have thought possible. "What are you up to?" she muttered. "You always know what time it is. You don't even *have* a clock in the kitchen."

"It's a test," Tillie whispered. "I read somewhere that they don't need clocks or watches."

Rafferty's easy, long-legged stride didn't falter. He glanced up at the sun and said matter-of-factly, "It's five forty-five."

"See! What did I tell you?"

At Tillie's triumphant whisper, Brandy groaned. "How did you do that?" she asked after Rafferty handed them each a bottle and eased down into Walter's chair.

His tawny brows rose. "Do what?"

"Tell the time by the sun."

He shrugged and took a long swallow of beer. "I told you I grew up near a Zuni reservation. I spent a lot of time there with one of my friends. His grandfather taught us a lot of the ancient ways.

"Ancient?" Tillie's eyes widened. She slid a delighted glance toward Brandy.

Rafferty's green eyes were hazy with memory. "Uh-huh. I was always fascinated by the night sky, imagining what it would be like to move through it." He grinned. "I had dreams of being an astronaut." He lifted the bottle to his lips and swallowed again. "Anyway, the old man taught us about the constellations, how the early people traveled with only the stars to guide them."

Brandy stared at him, barely breathing as one stark instant of doubt tore through her. Was he doing it deliberately? While Aunt Tillie was hanging on every word he uttered, was he teasing her, toying with her, knowing what she thought? Was it remotely possible that he *was*—

"I think I'll get the food ready," she said hastily. "Is it okay if we eat out here?"

Tillie nodded.

Rafferty touched Brandy's hand as she passed him, narrowing his eyes when she shivered. "Call me when it's ready, and I'll carry it out."

No, Brandy told herself as she scooped almond chicken into a shallow dish, it was *not* remotely possible. Rafferty Galen Travers was exactly what he looked like: a contemporary man, a successful man, a sexy and more than a little dangerous man. He wasn't being clever. He wasn't being devious. He wasn't being anything except a slightly nostalgic man sharing memories of his childhood. He was *not* an alien.

By the time she had the steaming food organized on the tray, she was thoroughly chagrined at her panicky withdrawal. Hoping that neither her aunt nor Rafferty had noticed, knowing she had no alternative but to face them, she closed the door quietly and walked toward the gazebo. Seconds later, she came to a dead stop, entranced by the scene before her.

While facing the music might be difficult, Brandy mused, it undoubtedly built character. Apparently there were other benefits, as well. Such as observing people when they didn't know you were around—as long as you did it quietly. Moving behind the cover of a lantana hedge, she crept closer, watching the petite woman's animated conversation with the man towering over her.

"*Rose,*" Tillie instructed with meticulous enunciation, touching one of the coral flowers entwined on the gazebo lattice.

Rafferty gazed down at her, dumbfounded, his green eyes riveted on her vivid face. "I—"

"Genus *Rosa.*"

"I—"

"It has prickly stems, alternate compound leaves and fragrant flowers."

"Aunt Tillie, I—"

"They need careful pruning and a great deal of care." Her expression darkened. "They are also plagued by mildew, aphids and—"

"Thrips," Rafferty finished.

Tillie blinked. "What do you know about thrips?"

"Only what my mother tells me."

"Mother?"

He nodded. "I told you about her when we had lunch the other day. She's a potter. She grows roses."

"And has thrips?" Tillie sounded thrilled.

He nodded. "From what she says, they're a constant problem."

Tillie turned to the lantana hedge and called, "Brandy! He really *does* have a mother. She has thrips!"

Stepping out from behind the bush, Brandy said dryly, "You needn't sound so pleased. I'm sure *she* isn't." She cast an oblique glance at Rafferty and wished she hadn't; the expression on his face defied description. Deciding that she didn't want to answer any of the questions he was about to ask, she said hastily, "The food's ready."

Later, Rafferty helped Brandy stack the empty dishes on the tray while Tillie trotted toward the house, her high-topped tennies making a crunching sound on the graveled walk.

"What did she mean, the phone's *going* to ring?"

Brandy grinned. She couldn't help it. Rafferty's hair was rumpled from running his hands through it, and he looked like a man hanging over a precipice, clinging to a rope that was slipping through his fingers.

"She meant exactly what she said. Just about the time she gets to the house, the phone will ring. Also, she already knows who's on the other end and that she wants to talk to them. Otherwise, she would have stayed out here."

"Why doesn't she just let her answering machine take a message?"

"She took it out. She said there was no sense in taking messages from people she didn't want to talk to in the first place."

"She's got a point." He leaned back in the chair, a brooding expression on his face.

Brandy laughed softly. "Cheer up. Aunt Tillie usually has this effect on people. You're doing better than most."

His eyes narrowed. "Most what? People? Men? Lovers?"

"You're not my lover."

"Yet."

The single word fell like a stone in a pond, dissolving laughter, sending ripples of tension through the small gazebo.

Sitting straighter in the high-backed chair, Brandy eyed him cautiously. "Rafferty, there hasn't been a man in my life—I'm talking about a serious relationship—for some time now."

"I know." Satisfaction gleamed in his jade eyes.

"How?" she challenged, diverted in spite of herself.

He lifted his shoulders in a small shrug. "The expression in your eyes, the way you move. Nothing about you says that you're taken."

"Taken!"

He grinned. "Don't get your feminine hackles up. You know what I mean. Involved."

Not sure she wanted to hear more, she asked anyway. "How else?"

"For starters, there's been no man trying to edge me out of the picture."

"Oh, for heaven's sake! The men I date are intelligent, mature men. They don't do things like—"

"The way I would if someone showed up on your doorstep now that I'm around," he finished smoothly.

"Rafferty! You have no reason to think—"

"I'll give you one." His voice stopped her in her tracks. "You're as wary as a half-wild cat around me. You shiver when I touch you."

"That's not because—"

"And when I kiss you, you make the most delicious sounds I've ever heard. Deep in your throat, like a purring kitten."

"Dammit, Rafferty, will you listen to me?" Brandy knew her face was flushed. It was one of the questionable joys of being a redhead, one she had learned to ignore. "There's not a man in my life because I don't *want* a man in my life right now. Are you with me so far?"

"All the way," he said mildly.

She glared at him suspiciously. "I don't want a man in my life right now because I have a business to run. I've just gotten it in the black and I intend to keep it that way. It's a full-time job. I have precious little spare time, and what I have is used on my class. I have no time for a man."

He nodded, waiting politely, deciding that now was probably not the best time to point out the holes in her logic. That men didn't have to have hairy knuckles dragging the ground to post a few "no trespassing" signs. That in spite of her hectic schedule, she was making time for *him*.

Brandy scowled at him, her blue eyes growing even more suspicious. He smiled blandly, knowing it would infuriate her.

"Well?" she demanded aggressively.

"Well, what?"

"Don't you have anything to say?"

He nodded. "Uh-huh."

She waited, tapping a pink fingernail impatiently on the glass tabletop. *"Well?"*

"Are you through?"

"Yes." She hissed the single word through clenched teeth.

"I understand."

She blinked. "You understand *what?*"

"That you're busy, that you don't have time for a man."

"Oh." She looked doubtful. "That's it?"

"No."

"No?"

"No."

"Pulling words out of you is like trying to make sense of the latest tax schedules," she snapped. "What else do you have to say before we permanently close the subject?"

"Just this. I'm not going anywhere. I'll be here when you're ready."

He didn't know for sure what ignited her temper. It might have been what he said, might have been his smile. Or it might simply have been nerves, the fact that she realized he was serious, that he really wasn't going away. Whatever it was, it was worth waiting for—and it was all for him.

Brandy's mass of coppery curls seemed to flame, and the color of her narrowed eyes darkened to a midnight blue. When her pretty lips parted and her hands clenched into small fists, Rafferty made himself a promise. Someday, someday *soon,* Brandy

Cochran would be his. All of her passion, her intensity, her tenderness, her humor. His.

He leaned back, savoring the notion, waiting for her to find her voice.

It didn't take long.

"Weren't you listening to a thing I said?" she demanded, stacking the dishes with more energy than care. "I said that I don't have—"

"I heard."

"Then why are you—"

"It's okay, Brandy. I promise."

Some element of his calm voice made her stop fussing with the dishes and stare at him. She believed him, Brandy realized with an even stronger flare of anxiety. He was the cause of her tension, the root of her problems, and yet he was promising that everything would be all right, and for some inexplicable reason, she *believed* him.

She must be crazy.

Brandy stiffened when Rafferty held out his large hand. She eyed it as warily as she would have a snake, telling herself that he could hold it there until it fell off, but she was not going to touch him. She lifted her gaze to his and slowly shook her head.

And damn his eyes, he *smiled*. Just as if she hadn't refused to touch him, just as if she wasn't trying to glare holes through him. He kept his hand where it was and smiled.

A man like that, Brandy decided, was either stubborn as a mule or too dumb to come in out of the rain. A man like that didn't know rejection when it reared up and poked him in the nose—or had enough confidence to ignore it. A man like that needed all the help he could get—or was cunning enough to give that impression.

The problem was, she wasn't sure which man he was, so she gave him one last halfhearted glare and slowly, reluctantly edged her hand forward. When her palm settled against his, his long fingers closed convulsively around her wrist. Instantly he loosened his grip. Then he turned her hand in his, lifted it to his mouth and dropped a kiss in her palm.

"It's okay," he promised again, closing her fingers over the kiss. Determined green eyes met startled blue ones in a glance as intimate as the soft caress. Brandy drew in a shaky breath, lost in the depths of silvery jade.

Tillie delicately cleared her throat.

When they turned, she was leaning against the rail, head tilted, looking for all the world like a colorful, bright-eyed bird. "Walter is rarely wrong," she said complacently.

Brandy snatched back her hand, flushing. Blurting out the first thing that came to mind, she said, "Don't tell me that was Uncle Walter on the phone."

Tillie shook her head. "It was Basilio. He wanted me to know that they would be late tomorrow. By the way, I want you both to come here on the sixteenth. A Saturday."

"What's the occasion?" Rafferty asked with an indulgent smile.

Gentle amusement shone in Tillie's blue eyes. "My surprise birthday party."

Chapter Seven

Kit stuck her head through the open door. "Got a second?"

"Sure." Brandy looked up from a catalog and absently stuck in a business card to mark her place before closing it.

Pointing to the thick book, Kit demanded, "Wait just a minute. Whose card is that?"

Brandy shrugged. "I don't know."

Giving a martyred sigh, the brunette inserted a fingernail next to the card and replaced it with a bookmark before giving it a cursory glance. "You'll be needing that for the holiday orders."

Brandy wrinkled her nose. "Yeah, I know. Someday I'm going to get organized," she promised.

"I did my part," Kit reminded her, reaching for a small box and briskly filing the card. "I got you this for Christmas last year."

"And I love it. I appreciate both the thought and the deed."

"If you like it so much, why don't you try using it? A system of some sort—however loose—can't hurt, you know. That way, we won't be tearing the place apart looking for addresses when you send in your next batch of orders."

Brandy ran her hands through her hair, pushing it back behind her ears. Narrowing her eyes, she said, "You haven't been talking to Rafferty, have you?"

"Me? Talk to the hunk? I haven't had a chance. Why?"

"No reason. Except that just the other night, he was suggesting much the same thing."

Kit dropped into a chair and stared at her boss. "About the shop?"

"My class."

"Ha! He's trying to organize *and* seduce you?"

"That's a loaded question, my friend."

"How about this one—has he seen your lunch-bag bookkeeping system? Since he's a high-powered CPA, he might be interested. Who knows, it might open new vistas for him."

"Are you kidding?" Brandy shook her head. "That's our secret. Only three people know about it. The two of us and—"

"Your long-suffering accountant. Who, if I remember correctly, devised the system out of desperation after trying to work with your old one."

"Don't knock it. It works. Once a month I take my bag of bills and receipts, cash register tapes and checkbook to him. He makes a copy of my check register, gives me back the book and sends me on my way. He's happy, I'm happy, and because I'm happy, you're happy."

Kit grinned. "You're trying to sidetrack me. I want to hear more about Rafferty and your class. Has he actually been there?"

"Three times." Brandy looked morosely at her friend. "The man's a glutton for punishment."

"What does he *do* there?"

"Mostly he sits in a corner and stares."

"At what?"

"My antics. All the moving around, the noise and confusion. And he makes notes."

Kit's smile grew broader. "Let me guess. He's critiquing you!"

"You got it."

"What a charmer. Then what?"

"Before or after he assures me that I'm a good teacher?"

"After."

"He explains how a little organization would enhance my efficiency."

"The monster." Humor lurked in Kit's brown eyes. "Did you tell him I've been saying that for three years?"

"I don't bother. He thinks it's an original idea." Brandy scowled. "He even wants me to organize my handouts."

"A cruel blow. He's *worse* than a monster."

"One suggestion was to separate them, put them in individual boxes."

"A loser. Definitely."

"I *have* them in a box," Brandy said in an aggrieved tone.

Kit grimaced. "I've seen it."

"What's the matter with it? It's sturdy."

"And big. Too big. All your papers slide around the bottom of it and get mashed. Then you toss in your tote bag and crush anything that's still in decent shape."

"You sound just like Rafferty," Brandy grumbled.

"You know, we've got a carton of boxes in the storeroom," Kit said thoughtfully. "Remember? The sales rep from L.A. left them with us several months ago."

Brandy nodded. "The shirt boxes with the fancy flowered designs. The ones that don't fit anything we have in the shop."

"Right. But they're a perfect size for your handouts," Kit said with mounting enthusiasm. "You could even pass them out to your students. And think how impressed Rafferty would be!"

"I'm not wasting my time trying to impress Rafferty."

"You don't *have* to try. I've seen him looking at you. Well," Kit persevered, "it's an idea. Think about it. I'll be happy to haul them out of the storeroom. By the way, how's the illustrious CPA getting along with our favorite aunt?"

"Swimmingly. She just invited him to a party."

Kit grinned. "Her annual surprise birthday party?"

"Yep."

"Oh, good! Am I invited?"

"Of course."

"Is it going to be the usual outrageous shindig?"

Brandy tilted her head, a wry grin turning up the corners of her mouth. "Have you ever known anything involving Aunt Tillie to be ordinary?"

"You've got a point. Do we bring gifts this time?"

"Nope. A wrapped gift is no challenge to Aunt Tillie. She knows what's in the package as soon as she touches it, and she hates trying to act surprised. Just a card and your presence will be fine. If you can't handle that, bring some flowers or a bottle of wine."

"Okay." Sheer anticipation rounded Kit's eyes. "Dare I ask? Are the Romero Brothers coming?"

"Oh, God." Brandy's eyes widened. "Don't even think it!"

"But they were the highlight of the party last year. It was a stroke of genius to invite them."

Brandy stared at her, aghast. "Kit, *nobody* invited them. Nobody *ever* invites them. They just show up."

"With guitars, trumpet, violin and sequined *charro* outfits?" Kit asked with a gurgle of laughter.

"Exactly."

"What is it they call themselves?"

"Cantores Sin Inqualidad."

"Singers without equal," Kit translated with a grin. "Well, that's honest enough. There's not another group in the world like them."

"Thank the Lord for small blessings," Brandy said piously. "I'm convinced that they're all tone-deaf. They can't sing and—"

"They definitely can't play. I especially remember the one with the trumpet."

"Trinidad," Brandy said with a sigh.

"Yeah. That man brought new meaning to the word awful." She tilted her head, puzzled. "What I don't understand is, if they can't sing and they can't play, why did they decide to become mariachis?"

"They liked the costumes."

Kit eyed her boss skeptically. "You're kidding, right? That's no reason to—"

"It was enough for them. You have to admit," Brandy said thoughtfully, "they do at least *look* the part."

The two women gazed at each other, recalling the lean men with luxuriant mustaches and flashing teeth, clad in the lavishly embroidered outsize sombreros, short jackets and tight-fitting pants with flared bottoms. Yes, they silently acknowledged, the five men *did* look the part.

"It doesn't make sense," Kit said flatly. "What experience did they have?"

"None."

"What did they do, before they climbed into *charro* outfits, I mean?"

Brandy swallowed. "They were kidnappers."

"What!" Curiosity quickly replaced shock. "Did they practice on anyone we know?"

"My cousin, Kara."

"The budding psychic? But how—"

"That's what I'm trying to tell you." Brandy fiddled with the pencil she had been using, then put it back down with a sigh. "You'd think that having Aunt Tillie would be enough for one family, wouldn't you?" she asked with a sigh. "But we got Kara, too. Anyway, to finance an orphanage in Tijuana, Kara was using her ESP to pick the winners at the racetrack. The Romero Brothers kidnapped her so she could teach them how to do it.''

"Do what?"

"Pick consistent winners."

"But—"

Brandy held up her hand. "Kara found out that they weren't really criminals but construction workers who were out of work. To make a long story short, she put them to work at the orphanage, and that's where they, their five wives and twenty-seven children now live."

Kit shook her head, obviously dissatisfied with several aspects of the tale. "I can understand—sort of— the kidnapping business. And having met Kara, I can even understand her putting them to work, but what I can't fathom is why they turned to music."

"I told you," Brandy said, her blue eyes gleaming with amusement. "They liked the fancy outfits."

"I guess I'm too practical," Kit sighed, getting to her feet. "Believe me, I'm going to look at them with new eyes the next time I see them."

Brandy picked up her pencil. "Well, I hate to be a spoilsport, but I sure hope it won't be at Aunt Tillie's party."

Long after Kit had left, Brandy sat staring at the open door. Fate wouldn't be so cruel, she finally decided, opening the catalog. It simply wouldn't dump the Romero Brothers on a plate already full with an aunt who was determined to unmask an extraterrestrial and a possible spaceman who was working with Immigration.

* * *

That evening Brandy perched in the center of one of the long tables and looked at her class. Twenty-five pairs of brown eyes looked back at her. They were amiable eyes, she reflected. Courteous, patient, tolerant eyes that seemed to be asking, "What is this strange little *gringa* going to do next?" She had a feeling that whatever she did, neither the eyes nor their owners would express more than mild surprise and willingness to follow directions.

Three of the students—Basilio, Adriano and Mega—were even more blasé. They were artists in Aunt Tillie's compound and, having survived daily encounters with the spritely lady, seemed beyond surprise.

Of course, what she was about to do wasn't all that cataclysmic, Brandy mused. Some people lived with structure and order every day of their lives. Her present course of action would only astonish those who knew her well.

And Rafferty.

At least he wasn't here to witness her capitulation, she thought, scanning the room and breathing a sigh of relief. She had spent a good part of the day considering Kit's suggestion—which had simply been a variation of Rafferty's theme—and had finally concluded that it was the obvious and sensible thing to do. But the decision had not been an easy one, and with Rafferty looking on, the implementation might have been awkward and a bit embarrassing.

But if there was one thing she was good at, Brandy reflected, it was facing facts. Especially when they were right under her nose and so big she couldn't see around them. It might take her a while, but she eventually saw the light.

It wasn't that she was stubborn, she assured herself. Or set in her ways. She was a reasonable person, amazingly so when one considered the mule-headed people she frequently encountered. She simply preferred to do things in her own way and in her own time. But was that so wrong? Didn't everyone?

And, yes, she admitted in a surge of nobility, she *did* have an instinctive resistance to authority—and to people who claimed that their way was the right way. Especially when she had a sneaking suspicion that her way was the *only* way.

But she wasn't stubborn.

Even when certain unnamed people attacked things that were near and dear to her heart—things such as the cozy clutter she chose to live with and the slight, very slight, lack of organization that kept her life interesting. Those people, in fact, simply didn't know what they were missing by living in a setting so sterile that everything not only had its place, everything was always *in* its place.

The creaking of a chair distracted Brandy from that satisfactory train of thought and brought her back to the present. Twenty-five pairs of brown eyes were still patiently trained on her, waiting.

"Oh." She looked around for her self-appointed translator, knowing the next task was beyond her rudimentary Spanish. "Basilio, would you explain something to the other students for me, *por favor?*"

She gestured toward the carton of gaudy gift boxes. "Tell them that these are for them. I want each person to take one and put his or her name on it. Then I want them to put all their papers in the box and keep them in there. It's very important that they keep them together, because we'll be using them later."

Basilio flashed a smile at her and turned to the task with enthusiasm. She was listening to the rapid flow of words when Rafferty walked in.

"... *muy importante,*" Basilio stressed.

Rafferty had on gray slacks and a navy blazer. His burnished hair was brushed back smoothly, his cheeks clean-shaven. He looked fresher at the end of the day than she did at the beginning, Brandy thought with disgust, watching him silently take a chair at the back of the room. She wondered briefly what it would feel like to look so perfect all the time, then shrugged. She wasn't into perfection. It required too much time and organization. Rafferty, however, was a living, breathing example of the successful, cosmopolitan, cool—

Her breath backed up in her lungs when he looked up and met her gaze. Well, she couldn't be right all of the time, she decided dazedly. But two out of three wasn't bad. And that was the best she was going to do, because there was nothing cool about the pure masculine hunger in Rafferty's green eyes.

"English as well as Spanish," she directed Basilio absently, staring at Rafferty.

"Your names, *sus nombres,* on the box," he directed, miming the action along one side. "For papers, *papeles.*"

Rafferty leaned back, holding Brandy's gaze, aware of the flare of anxiety in her eyes. He knew that a smile would reassure her, would ease her uncertainty, but at this particular instant a smile was beyond him. He was too busy coping with the tension stirring in his lower body, tension promising a blunt physical reaction that would put more than anxiety in her blue eyes.

He should be used to it by now, he thought grimly. It had happened often enough in the past three weeks, starting with the first time he walked into her shop.

He was a man who understood patterns, Rafferty reminded himself as he cautiously stretched out his legs. And it didn't take a Sherlock to figure this one out. Stated academically, it was simple: one look at Brandy, wherever she was, whatever she was doing, and his brain registered the fact that he wanted her. It was merely a civilized acknowledgment of his reaction to her.

Put like that, he decided, it sounded good. Real good. The only problem was that it didn't stay academic and it didn't stay simple. His body picked up the civilized message and interpreted it starkly and graphically, leaving him hurting and in a rotten mood.

So, no, dammit, he couldn't muster up a convincing smile.

"...*sí*," Basilio answered in response to an uncertain question, "*papeles importantes.*"

Rafferty, while half listening to the deep voice issuing directions, gazed at Brandy, concentrating on the coppery hair gleaming like fire against her deep green blouse. It was one of the reasons he dropped by as often as he did, he reminded himself. He could look as much as he wanted.

Her blouse was patterned after a man's shirt, which merely enhanced the sleek, feminine body it covered, and was tucked in the narrow waist of her white slacks. A single gold chain clasped her slender neck and disappeared inside the blouse.

She knew what he was doing, he decided lazily a few seconds later. And it made her nervous. Her spine stiffened and her fingers toyed with the gold chain until she caught herself and dropped her hand back to her lap. His mood lightened. It was nice to know he wasn't the only one acting like a hormone-ridden teenager. In fact, it made his whole day. And it would give *la profesora* something to think about when things got dull.

It was odd, Rafferty reflected wryly, how a little encouragement helped dissipate tension. Odder still, how hard he had to work for that bit of reassurance. She hadn't helped a bit, nor would she. Not Brandy Cochran. She made him fight for every inch. As it was, she'd be furious to know she'd given herself away. But she had, and he'd remember it. He'd have to, because as far as he could tell, her defenses weren't slipping at all. They were just as high and as tight as they'd been the day he met her.

But body language was a wonderful and revealing thing.

Brandy could glare all she wanted to, but he knew it wasn't just his gaze that had rattled her. When he had arrived, an entire roomful of people had been looking at her, and what had she been doing? She had been perched on the table, as much at ease as if she had been in her own living room.

Then he had walked in and she had begun to fidget.

No, lady, he thought exultantly, it's not the fact that I was looking. It's that I'm *here*.

When Brandy threw him another dark scowl, he grinned and glanced beyond her to the carton of colorful boxes. Then he looked at the man doing the talking and his smile faded along with his sense of satisfaction.

They were about the same age and size, Rafferty estimated, eyeing him with annoyance. The Mexican was as dark as he was fair, as dramatic as he was restrained. Good-looking, he allowed edgily. And he could talk the ear off a donkey.

Rafferty watched him sourly. The Latino was milking the situation for all it was worth, smiling at Brandy and practically doing backflips. After spending a few seconds wondering how good Brandy's Spanish was, Rafferty decided that it couldn't be too good, or she wouldn't have the Latin wonder running interference for her. If he was right, he mused, a flicker of pleasure stirring at the thought, she wouldn't recognize a short and earthy expression that would stop the jock in his tracks.

She might not, but everyone else in the class would.

And human nature being what it was, someone would eventually share the gist of it—if not the literal translation—with her.

But it might still be worth it.

"*Gracias*, Basilio," Brandy said mildly. "I think they understand."

For the next few minutes, while Brandy's students selected boxes and returned chairs, Rafferty stared at the tips of his gleaming loafers and contemplated his narrow escape.

Brandy wouldn't have been happy if he'd followed his impulse.

He realized with a sense of shock just how his life had changed in the past three weeks, how his priorities had changed. Because there wasn't much he wouldn't do to make one small, slender, sexy redhead happy and to keep her that way. He was so intrigued with the thought, he barely heard the flurry of goodbyes.

"What were you going to say?"

He looked up when the question drifted across the quiet room. Brandy was still sitting on the table, gently swinging her feet, looking highly entertained.

"Don't ask," he advised.

"That bad, huh?"

"Worse. Definitely not for your tender ears."

She laughed softly. "I could see it coming. For once, your face was very expressive."

"He was being a pain in the butt."

"He was helping me."

Rafferty got up and walked over to the table. Sitting next to her, he said, "Who's the pretty boy?"

"Pretty?" she asked, astounded.

"The one with all the words."

"Basilio? Pretty?" It was obviously an intriguing thought. Her brows drew together and she said, "Are you just a bit... out of sorts, tonight?"

"No." He lightly smoothed away her frown with his thumb. "I'm a bit jealous tonight."

"Jealous?"

He sighed sharply. "But I may *get* a bit out of sorts if you keep repeating everything I say. Who is he?" he asked again.

Brandy looked down, hoping to find inspiration in the crease of her slacks. Honesty was always an option, of course, and she had learned in the past few weeks that it was a trait highly regarded by Rafferty. It was a quality frequently linked to his name by others in the business community. Bluntness ran a close second. The general consensus had been, don't ask Rafferty a question if you can't handle the unvarnished truth.

So, did she try honesty? Sure. She winced, imagining his expression when she tried to explain about Basilio and the others. He was an artist, she'd say, and she had some of his paintings in her shop. Yes, he and several of the students worked on Tillie's property. No, she didn't know if they were in the country legally. Well, she hadn't really thought it was her place to ask. Yes, she supposed Immigration *would* be interested in the setup.

Giving a small shrug, Brandy abandoned honesty. "He's just a student in my class who speaks English a bit better than the others."

"Brandy? Excuse me?"

They both turned to face the door, where Basilio stood smiling.

"I forgot," he said, looking directly at her. "I will see you *mañana?* I have some stuff for you."

"Oh." She felt Rafferty stiffen beside her. "Uh...right." Only Basilio would call his exquisite paintings *stuff*. Only Basilio would have such abysmal timing. "Good night."

"At seven, as usual?"

She drew in a deep breath. Rafferty didn't move a muscle. "Fine. Good night, Basilio."

"At Señora Tillie's?"

"*Yes*. Good *night*, Basilio."

"*Sí. Buenos noches*." He flashed a final smile and disappeared as silently as he had materialized.

Without looking at the immobile man beside her, Brandy slid from the table, walked over to the large cardboard carton and silently piled handouts into colored boxes. She jumped when he followed her and began stacking the individual boxes in the larger one. He hadn't said a word. He didn't need to, she decided with a grimace. His silence was quite eloquent.

"So," she said brightly, "you speak Spanish."

He took the last box from her and put it with the others. "Yep."

"It was obvious that Basilio's grandstanding annoyed you," she persevered. "You'd have to be pretty good to keep up with him."

Shrugging, he said, "I told you where I grew up. It would have been hard *not* to learn."

"You obviously still use it."

"I make out." He picked up the box. "Ready?"

Brandy stalked over to the light and snapped it off. "Gee, this sure has been fun. Let's do it again some time," she said frostily, following him out to the car and opening the trunk. "Like maybe next year."

Rafferty tucked the box in and slammed the lid. "Glad you're enjoying yourself, because the evening's young. I'm following you home."

"The hell you are!"

"So we can talk." He opened her door and stood there, waiting.

"I don't want to talk."

"Tough. Get in, Brandy."

She got in. Rolling down the window, she stuck out her head and said, "I mean it, Rafferty. Go home, have something to eat, get some sleep. I don't need a lecture, and I don't need someone breathing down my neck. Good night!"

So much for having the last word, she reflected ten seconds later when his headlights appeared in her rearview mirror. They followed her all the way home, dropping away only when she turned into her garage.

He met her on the walk in front of her place, silently took the box from her, waited while she opened the door and followed her in. Ignoring him, she marched into the kitchen and turned the gas on under the teakettle. Rafferty leaned against the doorjamb.

"Herbal tea," she said tightly. "Yes or no?"

"Yes."

She dunked tea bags in two mugs and stood with her back to him.

"Talk to me, Brandy," he said quietly.

She whirled around, her eyes narrowed. "Why? So you can twist what I say and wonder what kind of crime I'm guilty of now?"

"What?"

She ignored his startled question and asked another of her own. "So you can go back to your office and write another report?"

"What?"

She snatched the whistling kettle off the fire and sloshed water in the mugs. "You heard me. The first day you came into the shop you as much as told me you thought I was a smuggler." She thrust the hot mug in his hand and sailed past him. "Don't swear at me, Rafferty. You know you did."

She dropped into her chair and curled her feet beneath her. "So I'm supposed to trust a man who's trying to put me in jail?"

Even in his rage, Rafferty managed to slam the mug down on a coaster. "Listen, lady—"

"I have a name. If you want to talk to me, use it," Brandy snarled.

"All *right*. *Brandy*. The only thing I've been trying to do—even before I met you—is keep you *out* of jail. How you can even think—"

"Think? *Think?*" She swallowed and said more quietly, "That's all I do. Think about the expression on your face when you looked around the shop, obviously expecting smuggled aliens to start leaping out of baskets. Think about perfectly innocent things, and how they can be misinterpreted—"

"All right," Rafferty said mildly, "then quit thinking. Just talk."

Brandy eyed him suspiciously. "We're right back where we started."

"Start with your friend, Basilio."

Brandy sighed. "It gets complicated," she warned.

Watching her over the rim of his mug, Rafferty said, "I'm listening."

"I didn't lie to you," she said abruptly.

"I believe you."

"Not exactly."

He sighed.

"He *is* a student."

Rafferty waited.

"He's also a wonderful artist. I have some of his paintings in the shop. You were admiring one of them the other day."

Blinking thoughtfully, he asked, "The wildflowers?"

She nodded. "That's the *stuff* he has for me. More paintings. Nothing sinister. No drugs. No aliens. Nothing illegal."

He thought about that. "Why at Tillie's place?" he asked abruptly.

Brandy winced. "That's the complicated part."

He took a swallow of tea. "I'm still listening," he finally said.

"No." Brandy set her mug down with a decisive click. "I think I'll have to show you. Will you go with me to Aunt Tillie's tomorrow?"

Chapter Eight

"Does Tillie know we're coming?"

Brandy lifted the piping hot pizza box and let the BMW's air conditioner cool her knees. Glancing at Rafferty's competent hands on the steering wheel, she said, "Does Pavarotti sing?"

"Did you call her?" he asked patiently.

"Not exactly."

"Then how does she know?"

"The way she *always* knows." She gingerly replaced the box on her lap. "She picked up my thoughts."

Staring straight ahead, he said expressionlessly, "You thought about it, and she—"

Brandy grinned. "I really love it when you do that."

"Do what?"

"Repeat something idiotic that I've said about Aunt Tillie and try to make it sound like it's a perfectly normal event."

Refusing to be sidetracked, he asked, "*How* did you think about it?"

"The same way I've always done it. I was very specific. I said to myself, 'Aunt Tillie, Rafferty and I are coming over at six tonight. Don't worry about dinner, we'll bring a pizza.'" She shrugged. "That's all there is to it."

He turned his head and stared at her. "*You're* psychic, too?"

"Keep your eyes on the road, Rafferty, there's a car coming! No, I'm not," she added more quietly as she leaned back with a sigh. "And believe me, I couldn't be more relieved. Besides, the psychic part comes in picking *up* the message. Anyone can send one. I think." She paused. "At least, most of us in the family can."

She crossed her arms and considered the matter. "I bet you could, too," she said slowly, remembering Tillie's certainty that she was "linked" with Rafferty—or Archer, as she still persisted in calling him.

He shook his head. "No I couldn't."

"It's no big deal," she told him, annoyed by his adamant tone. "All you have to do is *think*."

"There has to be more to it than that, otherwise she'd be inundated with messages from all over the world."

"I think she can filter out the stuff she doesn't want," Brandy said, dismissing his logic with a wave of her hand. "Why don't you try it?" she urged with mounting enthusiasm.

"No."

"Oh, Rafferty, don't be such a killjoy. Come on!"

"I wouldn't know what to think about," he said in a goaded voice.

"Good grief, we're not talking about a speech on national television here. Anything you'd say to her in a regular conversation will do. Ask her a question." She grabbed the flat box and steadied it when he turned onto Tillie's street. "I know! Ask her what kind of pizza she likes. Come on, Rafferty, we're almost there. Do it!"

He gave an exasperated sigh and muttered something beneath his breath.

"Don't talk," she urged. "Think!"

He eased the silver car up Tillie's wide driveway, stopping next to a battered pickup truck. "All right," he said, removing the key from the ignition, "I did it."

"What did you ask?" she inquired nosily.

"Exactly what you told me to." He gave her a long-suffering look, then opened his door and got out. Sticking his head back in, he said, "Are you happy now?"

Brandy smiled, enjoying the ruffled look in his green eyes. "I'll let you know in a minute," she murmured, handing him the pizza and reaching for her bag. When she joined him, Rafferty was examining the battered pickup with a grim expression. The paint job was mottled, ranging from primer gray to varying shades of yellow and red. "Tell me this isn't Tillie's," he demanded.

"It isn't Aunt Tillie's," she said obediently.

He slanted a skeptical look at her.

"I mean it. Really. It isn't."

"Archer! Brandy! Yoo-hoo!" Tillie waved from the front porch and trotted toward the car, her face radiant with excitement. "Pepperoni," she stated breathlessly, coming to a stop between them.

"Hmm?" Rafferty's assessing gaze had already returned to the dented, multicolored pickup.

"Pepperoni. It's my favorite."

Brandy folded her arms across her chest, leaned back against Rafferty's pampered car and made herself comfortable. Rafferty, she noted with interest, no longer seemed intrigued by the truck—even though he was still staring in that general direction. He stiffened. Stilled. He was absolutely, utterly still. After several seconds, he slowly turned his head and looked down at Tillie.

"What did you say?" he inquired politely.

"My favorite is pepperoni," she repeated, reaching out to touch the box he held. "Exactly what you got."

Brandy widened her eyes innocently when he flicked a stunned glance in her direction, but her voice reeked with satisfaction. *"Now,"* she said mildly, "I'm happy."

"You're late," Tillie informed them, leaning forward to sniff at the box. "But I knew you would be."

"How?" Brandy asked for Rafferty's benefit.

Tillie tapped the logo on the box. "They had a huge order for a party and were running late, but you had already left your shop so I couldn't call you." A look of mild vexation crossed her face. "This one-way communication is really very inefficient. I've thought so for a long time. Brandy, dear," she said earnestly, "don't you think if you'd just *concentrate* you could hear me? It's really quite simple. Kara took to it right away. Actually, without even trying."

Rafferty cleared his throat and said casually, "I think I'd better put the pizza in the oven. We don't want it to get cold."

"We'll come with you," Brandy said hurriedly.

"That's okay, I can handle it." He turned away, moving fast, saying over his shoulder, "Why don't you stay out here and enjoy the garden?"

"Rafferty!" She glared after him, and he lifted an acknowledging hand but kept moving toward the house.

"Brandy, he did it!" Tillie spun around and did an ecstatic little two step. "He talked to me before he got here! He *talked* to me! I knew it would happen. I *knew* it. What I didn't know was how long it would take before he would trust me enough to do it. But I've been working on it. Meditating, you know. Asking for guidance."

She touched her niece's arm, nudging her gently toward the house. "Let's not leave him alone. Now that we've made a breakthrough, we should keep right on—" She glanced up, puzzled. "You're awfully quiet. Aren't you excited? Just imagine, Brandy—" her blue eyes grew round with wonder "—I... spoke...with...an...alien."

"Aunt—"

"Who *knows* where this will lead?"

"—Tillie."

"We can exchange galactic information."

"I don't think—"

"He can show me his spaceship."

"—that he—"

"He might even take me to visit Walter!"

Brandy followed the older woman, listening with mounting horror. The only advantage this conversation had over the previous one, she thought numbly, was the fact that Tillie had temporarily abandoned efforts to turn a second niece into a psychic.

"Or take me home with him for a visit," Tillie continued blissfully. "He said he goes there two or three times a year."

Brandy gazed at the beatific expression on her aunt's pretty face and understood for the first time the full scope of what her other cousins had dealt with. Paying one's dues, Jana's rather cryptic expression, suddenly made sense.

But all of this simply because she had urged Rafferty to try an amusing little parlor trick? she asked herself in disbelief. A trick that the family had been doing for years? The retribution certainly seemed heavy-handed. Where was the justice? The logic?

She took another quick look at her aunt, the answer coming like the proverbial bolt of lightning. When you were dealing with a wild card like Tillie—a psychic who was also a flaming romantic and true science fiction devotee—there was no such thing as justice or reason. Things just were.

When they reached the brick walk, she stopped and clutched at Tillie's hand. "Aunt Tillie," she began gently, forcing her voice to remain calm, "there's nothing so unusual about what he did. He got through to you the same way I did. The same way that everyone in the family does.''

''Exactly.'' Tillie beamed. ''That's what I suggested in my meditation. I figured if *you* could do it, anyone could! I wanted to make his first attempt a simple one.''

''Thank you.''   \

The older woman tilted her head, studying her niece's wry expression. ''Oh dear, did I say something wrong?''

Brandy grinned and gave her aunt a swift hug. ''No. Absolutely nothing. It's just that I don't want you to think—''

''He trusted me, Brandy! Enough to break years of conditioning, enough to—''

''Aunt Tillie! It's not what you think! Really. Rafferty is just a man.'' Brandy faltered, remembering another time, another occasion, when Rafferty had murmured, ''just a kiss.'' A kiss that had turned out to be as overwhelming as the man himself. No, she admitted with reluctant honesty, there was no *just* about Rafferty. He might not be from another galaxy as Aunt Tillie believed, but he was definitely not *just* a man.

''That's what makes it so wonderful!'' Tillie tugged Brandy along with her in her haste to open the door. ''He's pretended to be a mortal for so long, I was afraid he really believed it. And you have to admit that he fits Walter's description.''

''Wait a minute.'' Brandy dug in her heels and brought them both to a stop. ''What description?''

"I'm sure I told you," Tillie murmured, edging closer to the porch.

"No," Brandy said definitely. "You didn't. The last thing I heard about was an arrow arcing through the sky."

"Well, Walter said—"

"I thought you told me he wasn't talking."

Tillie shook her head. "It was more like he had . . . gone into seclusion."

Brandy closed her eyes.

"Walter is a true Renaissance man," Tillie continued buoyantly. "He's always learning something new, and when he is, he doesn't like to be disturbed. But it was two days ago, or maybe three, he told me more about Archer."

"Like what?" Brandy asked faintly.

"He said that Archer is a practical man, analytical. That his approach in this life is direct—"

"This life?"

"—and uncompromising. That he sticks to facts and rejects illusions. Doesn't that sound just like an accountant?" She directed a blinding smile at her niece. "Of course we both know that it's just his earthly disguise."

Brandy clenched her teeth. I'll scream later, she promised herself. When I'm in bed and I can muffle the sound in the pillow.

"Underneath, he's . . . why he's . . ."

"What?" Brandy demanded, unable to stand the suspense.

"Unlimited," Tillie said simply. "He can do anything. If he wanted to, he could levitate, he could point at a building and destroy it. I once saw a movie where a man's eyes turned to lasers and melted iron bars.''

Brandy groaned. "Aunt Tillie, those were films. This is real life."

"I know. Isn't it *wonderful?*"

"Coward."

"You're right." Rafferty patiently held the tray while Brandy flipped a red-and-white-checked tablecloth over the table in the gazebo.

"You deserted me," she said dramatically, smiling in spite of herself. "Let me out there to cope with—"

"She's your aunt, not mine." He placed the pizza in the center of the table and reached for a large wooden salad bowl. "Well, did she talk you into it?" At her questioning look, he added, "Concentrating, tuning her in."

"I noticed you didn't stick around so she could talk to *you* about it."

"Damn straight, lady." He busied himself with paper plates and napkins. "My mama didn't raise a fool."

"Rafferty?" She waited until he looked around. "That business upset you, didn't it? I'm sorry. I just didn't think. We're all so used to it that I forgot how it would seem to... an outsider."

"No, sweetheart." He dumped the paper goods on the table and held out his hand. When she slipped hers in it, he gave a gentle tug and wrapped his arms around her. "I'm not upset. Nor," he added deliberately, "am I an outsider. We're soul mates," he reminded her when she looked up. "Remember?"

Brandy sighed and rested her head on his broad shoulder, savoring the peaceful moment. The sun washed the gazebo with warm light, and the only sound breaking the silence was the soft, throaty call of a mourning dove. She leaned against him, her lips curving in a small, very private, very feminine smile when his arm tightened around her waist.

He laced his fingers through her coppery hair and hesitated, momentarily distracted by the silken tangle. "I suppose I'm stunned," he finally said. "Not upset. I'm a practical man, Brandy. I rely on facts, on data. If I can't see, feel, taste or smell something, I have a hard time believing it exists."

"And now?"

He dropped a kiss on the top of her nose, smiling when she blinked. "You might say that Tillie has shaken some of my basic beliefs. Or disbeliefs."

Brandy winced. If he was disconcerted by what he had just experienced, how would he feel when he discovered that Tillie thought he was from outer space? *If* he discovered it.

She decided that she didn't want to know.

"Are we ready to eat?" Tillie asked, trotting up the wooden stairs. She studied them, her eyes bright with unabashed interest. When Brandy jumped, Rafferty's arms tightened, holding her where she was.

"Yes. You're just in time." Brandy wiggled free and moved around the table, hastily settling in one of the chairs.

"Are you all right?" Rafferty's low-voiced question brought her preoccupied gaze up from the steaming pizza. His concerned eyes held hers until she nodded.

Brandy took a shaky breath. Sure, she was all right. Just startled and a bit appalled at her sense of loss when she had moved away from the heat and strength of him.

"Are you sure?"

She nodded again, turning from his watchful gaze to look at her aunt. Tillie, dealing competently with stringy cheese and round slices of pepperoni, was radiating waves of sheer delight. Well, she had reason, Brandy reflected morosely. Not only had her precious alien "talked" to her, her niece was conveniently falling head over heels in love with the man. Spaceman. Whatever.

In *love?*

Brandy bit into the thick crust and chewed thoughtfully, considering the word. She was no starry-eyed adolescent; she was a discriminating woman, closer to thirty than she liked to think, who was... what?

Determined to have the time and space to put her business on a sound footing?

Lonely?

Stunned by the effect Rafferty had on both her heart and her nervous system?

Stubbornly resisting her aunt's machinations just on general principles?

All right, she conceded silently, she was a discriminating woman, still a few years shy of thirty, who was all of the above. She was also a woman in big trouble, because she was in love with a man who knew diddly squat about her present deception. A man of uncompromising honesty who would not be pleased to learn that his soul mate had been skirting the truth from the day she'd met him.

"Archer," Tillie said thickly, swallowing a piece of pepperoni, "we have to talk."

"We are talking."

"I mean, *talk* talk."

Rafferty studied her face for several seconds, then sighed. He finished his slice of pizza in two bites, washed it down with iced tea and wiped his mouth with his napkin. Resting his forearms on the table, he said bluntly, "If you mean mentally, no. What happened a while ago was a fluke, Tillie."

"You're sorry you did it?"

Looking at her downcast expression, he almost wavered. It was only the thought of the future that made him nod; he wasn't about to spend the rest of his life playing guessing games with a lady who talked to dead people. "I'm not into head games."

"You were just playing?"

He nodded again. "It was more in the way of an experiment," he admitted.

Tillie brightened. "Thank you."

Rafferty's brows rose. "For what?"

"For trusting me." When he just stared at her, Tillie added, "With your secret."

"Secret?"

"I know I'm the first, but I won't tell anyone," she assured him, darting a guilty look at Brandy. "No one at all."

Feeling a bit punch-drunk and wondering if he would ever understand the tiny woman across from him, he ignored her promise and moved on to the next hurdle. "And in spite of what I've seen lately, I think it's only fair to tell you that I don't believe in psychics."

"You don't?" She didn't try to hide her amusement.

"No." His voice was even firmer. He watched her slant another complicated glance at Brandy and wondered what was going on in that fascinating head of hers. He figured it wouldn't take long to find out.

It didn't.

"I think that's a very good story," she said approvingly.

He blinked. "It's not a story. It happens to be the truth."

"And I'd stick to it."

"I intend to."

"After all, denial might be your best protection," Tillie said thoughtfully.

"Denial?"

"Have another slice of pizza," Brandy said hastily, dropping one on his plate.

"Thanks." He turned to Tillie. "What do you mean, denial?"

"It's perfect camouflage," she assured him. "No one will suspect a thing. Just keep on doing what you've done for years and you should be fine."

Rafferty chomped on his pizza stoically, wondering if he had made his position clear. If her part of the conversation was any indication, he doubted it. On the other hand, he *never* understood her, but at least now, her expression was full of approval.

"Thank you. I think." He waited until the last of the pizza had been demolished before he turned to Brandy. "When are you planning to unveil the secret?"

Tillie, looking intrigued, glanced at her niece. "What secret?"

"The workshop."

"We can talk about it now?"

Brandy sighed. "I think it's time."

"Why couldn't you talk about it before?" Rafferty asked, gazing from one to the other.

Tillie's eyes widened. "Because you weren't supposed to know about it."

Brandy groaned when she met Rafferty's grim gaze. "Whatever I did," she stated firmly, "I did to protect my aunt."

"Who from?"

Tillie's voice was bright. "Why you, of course."

A few minutes later, walking across the deep yard, he was still frowning. "So you were protecting Tillie from me? Thanks a lot."

"Come on, Rafferty, in my place you would have done the same thing!" Brandy ducked under a trailing branch of bougainvillea and pushed open the back gate, revealing a tangle of bush and eucalyptus trees. "I didn't know you from Adam when you walked in and told me you were doing an audit for Immigration. I knew *I* didn't have anything to worry about, but then I thought of Aunt Tillie and her little artists' colony.''

"What made you think I'd be interested in it?''

She slanted him an apologetic glance. "It was the only thing that made sense. I thought at first that maybe you were using me to get close to her.''

He swore.

"Then I decided that you didn't know about it, but if you found out, you'd be interested—and *then* you'd use me to get close to her.''

He stared down at her, apparently fascinated. "You know," he said calmly, "your mind is as convoluted as your aunt's.''

"I had to take care of her," she insisted tightly. "If she was your aunt—''

"So what have we got here?" he interrupted. "Are they all illegal?''

Brandy pointed to the left, indicating a large wooden structure. "You're awfully calm about this.''

"Numb," he corrected. "So are they? Illegal?''

Shrugging, Brandy said, "I don't know.''

He stopped, clasping her wrist and bringing her to a halt beside him. "You've gone to all this trouble and you don't even *know?*''

"How often do you ask your clients if they're in the States legally?" she demanded. "I buy things from all over the country, and I've never yet asked a vendor to show me citizenship papers.''

He nodded briefly. "You've got a point." He looked at the low building and shook his head. "Come on. Let's get it over with.''

She took the lead on the narrow path, looking back over her shoulder occasionally. "Aunt Tillie originally turned the place over to Basilio, so he could paint, but he's a gregarious soul and couldn't stand the quiet. So one day he brought his wife out to visit and—"

"Wife?"

"Mmm."

"Kids, too?"

"Uh-huh." She looked around in surprise. "Why the interest?"

"No particular reason," he said with a shrug. "Then what happened?"

"Oh. He asked if one or two of his relatives could work along with him. Of course Aunt Tillie said they could."

"Of course." His voice was dry. "And how many are there now?"

"Eight or nine. I've lost count. But I've made out like a bandit, because most of them are my suppliers. You can't imagine how convenient it is."

He winced at her enthusiasm. "Try explaining that to Immigration."

"Rafferty!" Her eyes widened in shock. "You're not going to tell them, are you?"

He shook his head. "My report is done. My business with them is over. Even if it wasn't, I'd have no reason to mention Tillie or these people. The audit was based strictly on the reports I had."

"Oh. For a second there, you had me scared."

"That's not to say that they won't find out from some other source." He nodded toward a couple of the nearby homes. "Like the neighbors."

"I don't think that's a problem," she said confidently.

Rafferty touched her arm. "Listen." The gentle strumming of a guitar drifted across the still air, accompanied by a mellow baritone.

Brandy obediently stopped and tilted her head. "Nice, huh?" she said after a couple of seconds. "Someone out here is usually playing. If they're all really busy, a relative or two may come along just to entertain them. For all I know they may be practicing for Aunt Tillie's birthday party."

"The famous surprise party that she invited me to?"

She grinned. "The very one. It's become a tradition over the years. She loves parties, but trying to keep them a surprise was a lost cause, so now we just throw the biggest one we can manage." She took his hand. "Come on, let's see what the gang is up to."

They stopped in the doorway, and Rafferty took in the energetic scene in one swift glance. Basilio had an easel set up near a large window and, oblivious to the confusion, was producing another field of delicate wildflowers. A number of unframed paintings leaned against the wall near him. Sitting near the door, an old man weaving a basket looked up to tug politely on the brim of a straw sombrero. Two women worked in the far corner, one at a sewing machine, one on a small loom. Back in a small niche were oxygen and acetylene tanks topped with dials. Near them, a small man sat hunched over a countertop littered with silver medallions.

Rafferty sucked in a dismayed breath. This was no makeshift arrangement. There was nothing temporary about it at all. These artists had settled in—obviously with Tillie's permission and full cooperation—and had created an efficient and permanent working place. It was a scene guaranteed to trigger the hunting instincts of even a jaded Immigration agent. He hated to think what Farnum, his letter-of-the-law contact at Immigration, would make of it.

"Well, what do you think?" Brandy asked, smiling up at him.

Rafferty sighed. "Oh boy."

"As in 'hot dog'?" she asked hopefully.

"I was thinking more along the lines of 'you may have big trouble here, lady.'"

Three hours later, Rafferty poked the replay button on his answering machine. It whirred and recalled the pedantic voice of Clyde Farnum at Immigration.

"R.G., I just finished your report and found it quite thorough. However, there are one or two matters that I would like to discuss with you. Are you free on—" paper crackled while he obviously turned the pages of his calendar "—the sixteenth at eleven? If that's not convenient, call me. If I don't hear from you tomorrow, I'll be at your office on the sixteenth."

Rafferty stabbed the rewind button and sprawled on the long couch while the machine whirred and clicked. He studied the cool, serene room with critical eyes. It had been decorated according to his specifications, and until just recently, it had satisfied him.

It was cold, he decided moodily, trying to ignore the chill along his spine after listening to Farnum's message. Austere. It had no personality. Come to think of it, neither did Farnum. What did he want to discuss? Brandy? No. Rafferty shook his head. It couldn't be her. The report had covered that situation so thoroughly that not even Farnum could make something of it.

Well, he decided, surging to his feet, he'd find out on the sixteenth. Reaching out to turn off the lamp, he took a last look around. The place needed some color, he mused. Something bright, cheerful.

The place needed something yellow.

Chapter Nine

"Where did I put it this time?" Brandy muttered, groping through the untidy piles of notes on her desk without looking up from the file of invoices. "I had it just a minute ago."

"Is this what you're looking for?" Kit unearthed a banana clip from one of the heaps and held it in front of her boss.

"Thanks." Brandy took it and secured her hair on her nape. "What do you think?" she asked, eyeing her cluttered desk with disgust. "Will we make it by noon?"

"Since neither one of us intends to be late for Aunt Tillie's party, we *have* to be ready by noon. Don't fret," Kit said bracingly, "we've got a whole hour. It's not as bad as it looks."

"Really?"

"Really. I've got the front covered, so all you have to do is finish what you're doing. Darlene doesn't have classes today, so she's coming in any minute and will stay to close up." Kit ticked off the items on her fingers as she spoke. "Rafferty wants you to call him when you have a chance. The supplies you bought for the party are in boxes, ready to be put in the van."

Kit checked her fingers and stared blankly at her extended thumb. "Oh! Basilio called. Several of his relatives are in town and he wants to know if they can ride back with you in the van."

"Sure. That's fine," Brandy mumbled, looking down at the mass of papers before her.

"He figured you'd say that," Kit said dryly. "He said they'd be here before noon. Oh, by the way, Boss."

Alerted by the changing tone of her friend's voice, Brandy stiffened, then slowly lifted her head. "What?"

"Has Rafferty—or should I say, Archer—turned green or sprouted an antenna in the past two weeks?"

Stifling a groan, Brandy leaned back in her chair and stared at the ceiling. "Do I need this grief?" she demanded of the light fixture. "Was I crazy to think my best friend would offer a little sympathy when I told her my problems?"

"You have someone—an archer or whatever—that looks like Rafferty and you expect sympathy?"

"Is there no compassion left in the world?"

Kit perched on the corner of the desk and grinned. "Don't look so pathetic. Think how dull your life would be without Aunt Tillie. Mine, too. I haven't enjoyed anything so much since the time she took off for Dave's llama ranch looking for Uncle Walter."

Brandy gave a martyred sigh. *"Rafferty,"* she stated, emphasizing the name, "is no more from outer space than we are. He's a perfectly normal man who lives in a perfectly normal—if rather bland—condo, eats perfectly normal food, and—"

"Has perfectly normal male inclinations?" Kit asked hopefully.

"What *is* this?" Brandy jumped to her feet and prowled restlessly in the small space between the desk and the door. "A conspiracy to get me married?"

"Or something." Kit's gaze followed her pacing friend. "He's just so gorgeous, it's a shame to waste him."

"He's not being wasted," Brandy said through clenched teeth. "He's been a very busy man."

"Doing what?"

"Keeping *me* busy."

"Aha!"

"Driving me crazy."

"Better and better. Tell Mama all about it. Every sordid little detail." Her smile was wicked.

"He hasn't missed one of my classes," Brandy said abruptly.

"It's those sexy little boxes that got to him," Kit told her. "He has to go watch them."

"Don't look so pleased with yourself. That's not what he keeps his eyes on."

"Aha!"

"I wish you'd quit saying that," Brandy grumbled, dropping back into her chair. No, it definitely wasn't the boxes. Whenever she looked up, she met his lazy, speculative gaze. It didn't take a genius to figure out what he was watching with those silvery eyes. Eyes that were full of heat, full of promise. Full of determination.

"Then what?" Kit prompted.

"He follows me home."

"And spends the night?"

"Are you kidding? With Aunt Tillie tracking him twenty-four hours a day? Do you think I'm crazy?"

Kit slid off her perch and settled more comfortably in the other chair. "Is that the only reason?"

"You know it isn't," Brandy said with a wry look. "Until I can explain about Aunt Tillie's latest flight of fancy and be completely honest with him, we're not going anywhere."

"Then why don't you?"

Brandy scowled. "You make it sound so easy. I don't because the whole situation is so idiotic. It makes the whole family sound . . . weird. I keep hoping that Uncle Walter will come up with a reasonable explanation—"

"For an idiotic situation?"

"Yeah. Or something else to distract Aunt Tillie, so she won't be so preoccupied with Rafferty."

"Speaking of the devil," Kit said with a small smile as she got up, "you'd better call him."

Brandy picked up the phone and within seconds his receptionist was putting her through. "Rafferty? Hi, Kit said you called."

"Yeah." He sounded distracted. "Honey, I've got a minor problem here, and I might not make it to your place by noon. If I'm not there, go on without me and I'll meet you at Tillie's."

Brandy tilted her head, staring absently at the wall in an attempt to identify the emotion in his deep voice. Concern? Disgust? Giving up, she said, "Anything serious?"

"No." He hesitated. "Just an appointment I forgot about. Is there anyone to help you load that stuff in the van if I don't get there?"

"That's the least of my problems," she assured him, picturing Basilio's family arriving en masse at the store in less than an hour.

"Are you sure?"

"Even if I didn't have help, I'd manage. I haul things around all the time," she reminded him.

"I know, but—"

"Rafferty, it's *okay*. If you don't get here, I'll see you at Aunt Tillie's."

"Right."

"You *will* make it, won't you?"

"Absolutely. Brandy..."

"What?"

"Nothing. I'll see you later."

Now, what was that all about? she wondered, slowly cradling the receiver. Rafferty was not a man who wasted time being mysterious. On the contrary. He was painfully blunt, painfully direct. She had learned that the hard way, learned not to ask questions if she didn't want honest answers.

There was definitely something wrong with him. Usually when she talked with Rafferty on the phone, she had the impression that she was dealing with a large and unpredictable but good-natured cat. A cat who was willing to play but who would also pounce when you least expected it. A cat who was a trifle out of touch with his playful side but who seemed unexpectedly entertained by the process.

She gave the telephone a worried glance, then shrugged and fingered the file of invoices. Brooding about it wasn't going to do any good, she decided philosophically. She'd find out when she saw him. Until then, she had work to do.

An hour later, she gave a satisfied nod and said to the six men stowing boxes in the van, "I think that's it. *Gracias*. I'll be right back." She stuck her head in the door of the shop and when Kit looked up, said, "You don't see anything else I'm supposed to take, do you?"

Kit shook her head. "They got everything." She looked outside at the six men lounging by the van. All of them were lean, wearing jeans and dark knit shirts and creamy straw hats. "If you're crowded, a couple of them can ride with me."

Darlene strolled out of the back room, glancing at her watch. "You two better get out of here. You're never going to get the drinks and food set up in time."

Brandy said worriedly, "You'll be okay?"

"Fine."

"You'll come up after you close?"

"Yes."

"And you'll—"

"Anything! Just go!"

Brandy snatched her bag and trotted out the door with Kit right behind her. She hastily directed two of the men to go with Kit and shooed the others into the van.

Rafferty forced himself to sit still and listen to Farnum's precise voice. It was all part of the service, he reminded himself. Part of the hoop-jumping. When he slid a finger under his cuff and glanced at his watch, he hoped he wasn't being too blatant about it. He probably was, he mused. As Brandy had told him on numerous occasions, he wasn't big on subtlety.

But Clyde Farnum would have tried even Tillie's patience. He was a small, neat man who carried organization to the point of obsession. A meticulous man whose mental inflexibility matched his rigid posture, a man who latched on to loose ends, clinging to them with the persistence of a bulldog. The trait was particularly annoying to those who considered that they left no loose ends, Rafferty reflected, half listening to the punctilious flow of words.

"...fine audit. You are to be congratulated. It's unfortunate that the Cochran situation—"

Rafferty stiffened.

"—didn't hold water. Frankly, we could have used a solid lead. And it wouldn't have done either of us any harm to come up with one." Farnum's chin dipped closer to his chest and his hazel eyes looked out over the half glasses perched on his nose. "You could have earned a commendation, and I—"

"Tough luck," Rafferty said unsympathetically, "you'll have to find a lead to the *coyotes* somewhere else, because she's so clean she squeaks."

"Pity," Farnum murmured, slipping off his glasses and tucking them neatly in his breast pocket. "A young businesswoman, probably well known in town, the publicity would have been . . . gratifying. I would like to see her shop, just to satisfy my curiosity."

Gratifying? Rafferty surged to his feet, wondering how gratified the twerp would be to have his neck wrung. "It's right in town," he said briefly. "Easy enough to find. As a matter of fact, I'm going that direction now. If you didn't have your car, I'd offer you a ride," he added in a brusque tone.

Farnum locked his briefcase and stood up. "That's nice of you. And since I walked here from town, I'll take you up on your offer. Oh, yes," he said, responding to Rafferty's surprised glance, "I walk at least five miles a day." He patted his flat midriff complacently. "Have to stay in condition. You never know what could come up in the course of a day's work."

Rafferty led the way to his car, not liking the direction his thoughts were taking. Clyde Farnum, fussbudget and royal pain in the neck, unlikely as it seemed, appeared to be a gung ho mercenary type at heart. If that hopeful gleam in his eyes was any indication, he was probably a self-taught master of guerrilla tactics who would sell his soul for a chance to play Rambo.

Rafferty glanced over at his companion as he drove down the wide street. The more he considered the idea, the less he liked having Farnum anywhere around

Brandy. He'd point out the shop without even slowing down, he decided, then take him to wherever he had left his car. And maybe, if he was lucky, somewhere along the way, Farnum would stop talking.

"Diet and exercise," Farnum said, summing up his monologue. "That's the secret of staying fit. And no alcohol. The stuff will kill you . . . of course, I have no problem with it . . . never drink it . . . learned my lesson early . . . I don't metabolize it in the way most. . . ."

"There it is," Rafferty murmured. "Down toward the end of the block. That one." He pointed. "With the green-and-white awning. In fact, that's Miss Cochran coming out the door."

Farnum squinted. "The one running?"

"Yeah. The first one." The sexy redhead in yellow. "The other one's her assistant."

"Slow down, Travers, there's something odd . . ." Farnum stiffened. "Look at that! In broad daylight, right in the middle of main street!"

"What?" The gray luxury car in front of Rafferty stopped, waiting for a sedan to pull out of a parking space. Rafferty stopped and looked where the other man was pointing—right at Brandy and Kit.

"By God!" Farnum sounded awed.

"What?"

"She's doing it! Right here in front of us. We're witnesses, Travers!"

Rafferty watched Brandy gesture toward Kit's car and two of the six men by the van obligingly trot in that direction. Turning to the excited man beside him, he asked mildly, "Doing what?"

"Travers," Farnum faced him, hazel eyes narrowed with zealous determination, "we can break this thing. It's the chance of a lifetime."

"What thing?"

"This is a *coyote* drop if I ever saw one. Look at her! She's practically pushing those four in the van! Get closer, closer!"

"There's a car in front of me," Rafferty reminded him.

"Damn." Farnum reached down, fumbled and withdrew something from his briefcase.

"What's that?"

"A camera. I always keep one on hand, just in case something like this comes up." Farnum held it to his eye and snapped through the windshield. "It has an automatic zoom so it should do the job," he mumbled.

Rafferty stared at him. "I don't believe this."

"Believe it, Travers." Farnum kept snapping, concentrating on the van, then moving to Kit's car. "We're going to break this thing wide open!"

"Farnum, there's probably some perfectly simple explanation for what they're doing," Rafferty began, straining to keep the impatience out of his voice. Farnum was already leaping to conclusions; it wouldn't improve the situation by alienating him.

"Yeah, like maybe they got the merchandise late—"

"Merchandise?"

"Those six guys. And they have to pass them on now instead of at night the way they usually do. Hey, they're taking off!"

"I figured they would."

"Travers," Farnum pointed a bony finger at the two vehicles passing in the opposite direction, *"follow those cars!"*

Rafferty considered the matter while Farnum leaned over the back of the seat and took pictures through the rear window. He could drop Farnum at his car, but that wouldn't end the matter. With his bulldog tendencies, Farnum would involve Brandy, her shop, Tillie and her artists in a situation that could take weeks to clear up. No, he decided, swinging around the gray BMW and pulling a quick U-turn, it would be safer for everyone to keep Farnum close, to introduce him to Brandy and show him just how innocent the whole setup was. Safer, he reflected grimly, assuming that all of Tillie's protégés had the papers Farnum would undoubtedly ask to see.

"Good move, but don't get too close." Farnum turned around and slid back down in the seat. Securing his seat belt, he leaned back and briskly rubbed his hands. "I got their license plates in the last ones."

"Look," Rafferty said, his voice barely civil, "you're way off the track with this. I checked her out—"

"Don't blame yourself, Travers. Anyone can be fooled."

"I wasn't fooled. What I'm trying to—"

"They're turning! Don't lose them."

"I know where they're going," Rafferty said calmly. "We won't lose them."

"Ah, so you *have* kept your eye on them."

"You might say that."

"Good man." Farnum ran a hand through his neatly brushed sandy hair. "You've got good instincts, Travers. You must have had a gut feeling that something was—"

"*Farnum. Listen* to me! You're wrong about this. I'm going to take you there and prove it to you. I'll introduce you to everyone, you can ask all the questions you want, and you'll see that I'm right. Nothing could be simpler."

Farnum stared straight ahead, keeping his eyes on the two cars. "Don't get too close," he directed. "And when we get there, pull over. Give them time to get inside."

Rafferty shook his head in exasperation. It was going to be a long afternoon, he reflected grimly.

Kit pulled into Tillie's driveway and stopped behind the van. While the men were hauling boxes into the house, she said, "I thought I saw Rafferty's silver bullet behind us."

Brandy looked down the tree-lined street. "I don't see him, and I don't have time to wait. Come on, we've got to get the punch made." They stepped onto the brick walk, their heels tapping briskly, when a hideous sound shattered the silence.

Brandy jumped. "What on earth? It sounds like a pig being slaughtered!"

"Or bad car brakes."

The two women stood frozen. The din picked up volume, then faded to a whimper. It was soon joined by a wavering whine, reminiscent of fingernails scratching a chalkboard.

Kit's hand rose to her throat. "Be still, my heart," she whispered exultantly.

Brandy shook her head. "No," she said calmly, then flinched when another squeal made the fine hair on her nape stand up.

Kit gave her an ecstatic hug. "It *is*. Brandy, the Romero Brothers are here!"

Chapter Ten

"Who are all those people? And whose house is it?" Farnum asked, alternately staring out of the window, taking pictures and scribbling notes in a small book. The two men were still seated in the car, parked down the street from Tillie's house.

Rafferty shrugged impatiently. "Friends, neighbors, relatives. I don't know. The house belongs to Miss Cochran's aunt."

"But why today?" Farnum's puzzled gaze followed another couple to the front door of the white house. "Why would Miss Cochran arrive with the—"

"Don't say merchandise," Rafferty advised through clenched teeth, spacing the words for emphasis.

"—men the same day that all these other people are pouring in?" Farnum's eyes narrowed to slits. "It must all be part of a master plan. Look how many of the men are dressed like those six guys were—jeans, dark shirts and straw hats. I tell you, Travers, they're going to pull a switch."

He hit his thigh with the side of his fist. "That's it, they're going to slide those six out with some of the guests! This thing is bigger than I thought, Travers. And it's highly organized!"

"Farnum," Rafferty said wearily, "it's a birthday party, and knowing the people involved, I doubt if it's organized at all."

"How do you know it's a birthday party?"

"I was invited."

"Invited." Farnum repeated the word slowly, testing it, searching for hidden motives. "Just how well do you know these people?" he finally asked.

"Quite well." Rafferty yanked the keys from the ignition and opened the door. "Well enough to know that they're not involved in anything illegal. And well enough to know that I'm missing a good party." He got out and took off his jacket and tie. Leaning in to drape them over the back of his seat, he said, "You can sit out here taking notes and pictures as long as you want, but I'm going inside. If you want to straighten this out, come in and let me introduce you to Miss Cochran."

Before Farnum got out of the car, he locked his briefcase, tucked his notebook in the pocket with his glasses and put the slim, black camera in another. "I'm not invited," he reminded Rafferty as they approached the brick walk.

For the first time in several hours, Rafferty's expression lightened. "It doesn't matter."

Just as they reached the small porch, Tillie, resplendent in a gauzy purple, pink and chartreuse outfit, threw open the screen door. "Archer!"

Farnum looked over his shoulder, a perplexed expression crossing his face when he saw no one behind them.

Purple feathers, held in her silvery curls with a comb, bobbed over one eye when Tillie moved her head. "Why on earth were you sitting in that car? We've been waiting for you. And you've brought a friend." She patted Farnum on the arm when Rafferty introduced him, soothing him with a smile when he jumped. "Are you from . . . New Mexico, too?"

Farnum shook his head, speechless, eyeing her with fascination.

Tillie turned her bright gaze back to Rafferty. "From another plan—place near yours, I suppose."

"Search me," Rafferty muttered, following her into the room.

Right on his heels, Farnum hissed, "Who's Archer? You didn't tell me it was a costume party. I don't like masquerades."

"Relax. She always dresses like that."

Farnum blinked. "You're kidding."

"Mr. Farnum—" Tillie led him toward the backyard "—come meet my friends. Very nice people. Of course, some of them don't speak English, but they have beautiful smiles! Archer, Brandy is in the kitchen."

Rafferty left Farnum to his fate and veered to the right, halting at the kitchen door. Brandy had her back to him, dividing her attention between Basilio and a brimming punch bowl. Her hair was piled on top of her head, held in place by a couple of wicked looking combs, but wisps of fiery hair were already straggling down and softly brushing her nape.

"Basilio," she said crisply, "I don't know what you're up to, but if you've put anything in that fruit punch, I'll have your head."

"Me?" The artist's dark brows shot up, and he managed to look both wounded and impossibly innocent. He gave an elaborate shrug, keeping one hand tucked neatly behind him. "I just came to help."

"Fine. I can use all I can get. How about carrying out the punch bowl? And keep an eye on it. I don't want any hard stuff poured in it."

"What can I do?"

Brandy whirled at the sound of Rafferty's deep voice, a smile lighting her face. "Oh, hi." She tilted her head, watching as he unbuttoned the neck of his pale shirt and rolled his sleeves to his forearms. "Did you just get here?"

"Yeah. I got held up."

Behind her, Basilio quietly buried an empty tequila bottle in a plastic trash bag, then picked up the punch bowl and edged between them, giving the other man a quick grin.

"What can I do to help?" Rafferty repeated. Later, he promised himself. He'd take her up on the warmth shining in her blue eyes. Later, when they were alone. When they—

"Help?" Brandy blinked up at him. As always, he looked lean and elegant. A bit predatory. And wonderful. "Oh. Help. Yes. You can... check the tables outside and see if any of the dishes need to be refilled." She cleared her throat and turned back to the counter.

"Okay." Smiling, he bent his head and touched his lips to the soft curve of her nape. "Whatever you want." When she jumped and looked at him over her shoulder, wide-eyed, he smiled again and dropped a second kiss next to the first. "Whenever. Wherever."

"Archer!" Tillie whirled into the kitchen followed by purple tendrils of fabric. "Your nice friend is fitting right in. He's interested in everybody. And everything. I told Basilio to show him the workshop. Don't you think he'll be impressed?"

Rafferty swore. "I'd better get out there."

She blocked his path. "He's just fine. Basilio gave him some fruit punch and now he's taking pictures of the party."

Brandy cut some more broccoli for the vegetable platter before looking up. "Basilio is?"

Tillie shook her head. "No, Clyde is."

"Who's Clyde?"

"The man from Immigration," Rafferty said grimly.

"What!" Brandy's eyes widened. "*Immigration?* How'd he get here?"

Tersely Rafferty told her.

Stunned, she said, "And he thinks that I'm—"

"Part of a chain, bringing illegal aliens into the country," he finished.

Brandy tossed the small knife aside and dried her hands. "That's it!" she declared, a militant gleam in her eyes. "I've really had it with these government types. If it isn't forms up the kazoo, someone's sneaking around taking pictures at a family party. I'm going to go set that idiot straight."

"Brandy." A grinning Kit stuck her head in the door. "Come out here. You've got to see this. Hurry!" She withdrew her head, but before the screen door swung back, it was caught and opened again.

"Miss Tillie," Clyde Farnum acknowledged politely, bracing himself in the doorway. "Nice party." He blinked. "Very nice party. May I use your telephone?" His gaze drifted to Rafferty and slowly focused. "Hi there, R.G."

"Of course you may." Tillie smiled warmly and gestured toward the other room. "I'll show you where it is."

"Nice of you, Miss Tillie." Farnum detached himself from the doorjamb and took a cautious step into the room. "Nice people. Nice workshop out there. Nice fruit punch." He listed toward the right, hesitated, overcorrected, and leaned toward the left. "Verrry nice fruit punch."

"Clyde," Rafferty extended a hand, then withdrew it as the other man straightened, "how much of that stuff have you had?"

Farnum blinked but didn't stop moving toward Tillie. "Don't know," he finally decided. "Got real thirsty waiting out there in the car."

Brandy watched his unsteady departure, then turned to Rafferty. "*That's* the menace from Immigration?"

He nodded, staring at the empty doorway, his brows drawn together in a frown.

"Brandy," Kit called, "hurry *up*."

Tillie bustled into the kitchen, her eyes bright with excitement. Shooing Brandy and Rafferty ahead of her, she said, "Trinidad is going to play a song for my birthday."

Brandy swallowed. "Trinidad?" she said weakly.

Her aunt nodded. "With the others. And I don't want to miss a bit of it. He's so talented! They all are."

Brandy slid her an astonished glance, but before she could think of anything to say they had joined the others. Chairs were scattered around the yard and Tillie headed for three nearest the musicians.

The five men were still lean, mustached and darkly attractive, Brandy noted, settling between her aunt and Rafferty. They still wore their black, elaborately embroidered and sequined outfits with swaggering grace. They still stood too close and bumped into each other with their matching, equally elaborate, outsize sombreros.

They leapt to the raised floor of the gazebo with a clatter of boot heels, smiled at their audience and jostled each other with their elbows until they had sufficient space for themselves and their instruments. When they were settled, the one with a guitar strapped across his chest stepped forward.

"*Señoras y señores,*" he said, "ladies and gentlemen, we are the Romero Brothers, the *Cantores Sin Inqualidad.* the Singers Without Equal." They all bowed smartly while the audience cheered and whistled.

Rafferty leaned back, murmuring, "They've already got the audience hooked. They must be good."

Brandy watched the men untangle their instruments and glower at each other. "Let's say they're . . . unique."

The spokesman continued. "First, with the *trompeta* is Trinidad!"

More applause and whistles filled the yard when Trinidad leapt forward and held up his trumpet.

"And on the *guitarrón*, Pepe!"

More cheers. Pepe's gold tooth flashed as he displayed an enormous, pregnant-looking guitar.

"Gabriel!"

Stamping feet and a few olés greeted the violinist.

"Sancho with his *vihuela!*"

Hoots and more applause for Sancho and a mandolin lookalike.

"And I," he clutched his guitar and smiled modestly, "am Domingo!"

All the brothers bowed again in the uproar that followed. When the din quieted, the five men were engaged in a heated argument.

"Don't they want to sing?" Rafferty murmured, leaning closer to Brandy.

"They always want to sing," she said stoically. "Or play. They just can't agree *what* to sing. When they get that settled, then they can't agree when to sing it."

Domingo struck a resounding chord on his guitar, stilling the murmuring audience.

Rafferty stiffened. "I don't know much about music, but I'll bet my new computer that he's just invented a new chord."

"I don't bet on sure things," Brandy whispered, smoothing down the hair on her arms and wondering if Domingo had ever heard of tuning instruments.

"In honor of Señora Tillie's *cumpleaños* today, we, the Romero Brothers, have written her a song. All in English," he added proudly. "It's called 'Good Wishes for a Year.'"

The five men inhaled, holding the air until their eyes bulged. When Pepe stamped his booted foot, they exploded into what resembled a syncopated Gregorian chant.

"January one is New Year's Day," Domingo bellowed while Gabriel sawed his violin and Trinidad fumbled with the keys of the trumpet.

"Good wishes on New Year's Day," Pepe, Gabriel, Sancho chorused. Trinidad coaxed a thin bleat from the trumpet.

"January twenty-one is Martin Luther King Day," Domingo bawled over the clashing of four stringed instruments.

"Good wishes on Martin Luther King Day," the others chorused.

Tillie beamed.

"I thought Tillie said they were talented," Rafferty said in a stricken voice.

"Aunt Tillie is tone-deaf."

"February twelve is Lincoln's Birthday," Domingo thundered, fingering a discord that wrung a groan from Rafferty. Trinidad's cheeks bulged, then his eyes, but the trumpet was silent.

"Good wishes on Lincoln's Birthday," wailed the chorus.

Domingo wiped his brow with a handkerchief and took a breather. Trinidad, still blowing, turned to look at his brother just as the trumpet let out a bloodcurdling trill. Domingo jumped and almost lost his hat.

Farnum lowered himself gingerly into the chair next to Rafferty. "I called for a backup unit," he muttered. "They'll be here any minute."

"What?"

Rafferty flinched as Domingo consulted a notepad and bellowed, "February thirteen is Ash Wednesday."

"I'm going to have them take those five first. If what they're doing isn't against the law, it should be."

"Good wishes on Ash Wednesday," Pepe, Gabriel and Sancho brayed, flailing their instruments.

"We're only in the middle of February," Rafferty said numbly.

"February fourteenth is Valentine's Day," Domingo persevered, visibly wilting. Farnum stretched out his legs and hummed along, a dreamy smile on his face.

Rafferty's lips brushed Brandy's ear. "Your friend Basilio spiked the punch and *my* friend is stewed to the gills."

"Oh lord. I'll go make some coffee."

"I'll come with you," he said hastily as the three men chorused their response.

"Oh no you don't." She jumped to her feet and whispered, "I thought of it, I get to do it. You stay here and enjoy the music."

Winding her way through the chairs, Brandy reached the covered walk just as Domingo thundered, "February eighteen is George Washington's Birthday!"

Twenty minutes later Brandy walked out with a steaming coffee mug. The first thing she noticed was the quiet. The early-bird crowd had thinned considerably. The most obvious absence, and least lamented, was that of the Romero Brothers. Blissful silence reigned.

Brandy looked around and did a rapid tally. Most of the family members were coming later, but even so there were a lot of faces missing. All of her students had disappeared, Basilio and his family were gone, there was no Farnum, no Rafferty, no Kit and no Aunt Tillie.

Walking over to one of the tables, she slid into a chair opposite a tall, bald man and his attractive gray-haired wife. Mr. and Mrs. Franks, Tillie's neighbors.

"Where is everyone, Glen?"

He leaned back, intelligent gray eyes taking in the steaming coffee and her bewildered expression. "How long were you inside?"

She shrugged. "Fifteen or twenty minutes, I suppose. I had to run to the store for some coffee."

"We were raided, Brandy!" Corinne Franks was highly amused.

"Raided?"

"Immigration," Glen said succinctly.

"That twerp!" Brandy's eyes flashed.

"You should have seen it, Brandy," Corinne said. "First they took the Romero Brothers and some poor man who was—"

"Soused," her spouse supplied.

"Then while your Mr. Travers and Basilio talked to the officers, Tillie sent your students off on a paper hunt."

"Paper hunt?" Brandy stared at her blankly.

"She had the right idea," Glen said, the corner of his mouth kicking up. "Unfortunately none of us can speak Spanish, so she just waved her arms and told them they needed papers."

Brandy groaned. "What'd they do?"

"They *like* Tillie," Corinne said earnestly, "and they wanted to please her. So they brought sales receipts, newspapers, magazines, anything they could find."

"And?"

Glen took up the tale. "The officers thought they were being less than cooperative and took them all away."

"So your Mr. Travers assured us that his lawyer would be on the case by the time they got wherever they were going. He asked us to hold down the fort while he went with them and straightened everything out. Tillie said she was going with Archer—whoever that is—and Kit just got swept up with the rest of them."

Glen studied Brandy's face. "A lawyer isn't a miracle worker," he stated quietly. "If Basilio's family and your students have papers, someone better get them down there."

Brandy got up. "My thought exactly. Will I see you later?"

Corinne grinned. "We'll be here."

* * *

Two hours later Brandy pulled up in front of a large, official building and opened the back door of her van. Two men emerged and followed her, balancing an enormous carton between them. She asked questions, followed direction and walked down a long hall. At the end, on one side, was a door with a small window.

She stood on tiptoe to peek through the glass and froze. There they were, all of them. The Romero Brothers lounged in one corner, playing cards, their huge sombreros on the floor beside them. Their instruments were nowhere in sight. Farnum was stretched out on a bench, still sleeping. Basilio, his family and her students were quietly visiting.

No one looked alarmed. Tillie and Kit were pouring over a paperback book, having a lively discussion. And "her Mr. Travers" was sitting in a chair perched on its two rear legs managing to look extremely competent and devilishly elegant. He also looked very thoughtful.

He was probably wondering how he got mixed up with such a bunch of lunatics, she thought morosely, turning to the office across the hall. And how fast he could get away when they opened the doors.

She knocked politely on the doorjamb and waited until the two men looked up. One was in uniform, the other had steel-gray hair and was wearing a dark, pin-striped suit. She turned to that one and said brightly, "Are you Rafferty's lawyer?"

Two hours later an officer opened the wooden door with the window. Brandy directed her students to the two men standing by the large carton so they could get their colored shirt boxes.

Tillie wandered out, frowning thoughtfully, followed by a grinning Kit. "What do we do for an encore?" her friend asked.

"The van's in the parking lot," Brandy told them. "We've got transportation arranged for everyone else."

"The Romeros have to get their instruments. The officers confiscated them at the party." Kit laughed softly. "They said they'd be doing the civilized world a favor if they kept them."

Brandy didn't hear her. She was staring at the last occupant in the room. Rafferty ambled over to the door and just stood there, watching her.

"You were right," she said abruptly. "Being organized helped. They all thought Basilio said to keep their important papers in the box, so when I went to each house it was a simple matter to find them. And yes, they all had papers. Even the Romeros were here legally for the day."

Tillie blinked. "Were you worried about that? I *told* you that we were all exactly where we're supposed to be."

Keeping her eyes on Rafferty, Brandy challenged him softly. "Anything else you want to know?"

He cupped her cheek with his palm, brushing her soft, stubborn, lower lip with his thumb. "Yeah. When are you going to marry me?"

"Whatever happened to romance?" Kit mourned, watching Brandy navigate through town as they headed back to Tillie's. "The man asks you to marry him, then rides back with his lawyer?"

"I invited Mr. Castle to the party," Tillie said absently. "Archer wanted to show him the way."

"Aunt Tillie, are you all right?" Brandy directed a concerned glance in the rearview mirror. "You look like something's bothering you."

"Yes. I am. Something is."

Brandy's voice gentled. "What's the matter?"

"Who, not what," Tillie muttered. "*Walter* is the matter."

"Why? What's he done?"

Tillie plucked at her gauzy dress. "He's covering something up. For some reason, he doesn't want me to believe what he told me about Archer."

"What do you mean? Are you saying that now he's telling you that Rafferty *isn't* from outer space?"

Tillie nodded.

"Why would he change stories? It doesn't make sense." As if anything Uncle Walter did made sense.

"He says he didn't," Tillie told her indignantly. "He *says* that I misunderstood him. That he has become very interested in astrology and was simply giving me some pointers about the various signs. But *I* think that something big is happening up there, and someone found out that he told me. I think Walter is covering his—" She coughed. "That he's changing his story to protect himself."

Brandy ran a hand through her hair, dislodging one of the combs. "I don't understand any of this."

"What she means," Kit said in a carefully controlled voice, "is that now Walter insists he told her that you were going to meet a Sagittarian."

"A *what?*"

"You know, someone born between November twenty-second and December twenty-first."

"I don't believe this."

"I don't, either," Tillie said stubbornly.

"Sagittarians," Kit continued serenely, "are—according to the book Walter conveniently placed back there in that room for us—analytical and determined. Their approach to life is direct and uncompromising. In other words they are just as blunt as they are honest. They stick to facts and reject illusion."

"That doesn't mean any—"

"Their reigning planet is Jupiter."

"Well, that still—"

"And," Kit gently delivered the coup de grace, "their symbol is the archer."

"Wait a minute," Rafferty said, tightening his arm around Brandy's slim waist. The party had finally ended and they were in her condo, stretched out on the couch. Brandy's head was resting on his shoulder, and she had just finished telling him the most incredible story he had ever heard. "You're saying that Tillie thought I was from outer space?"

"Right."

"That's what all that business about the arrow in the sky was about?"

She nodded. "Right."

"And you knew it but you didn't tell me?"

"Right." She looked up, her eyes laughing at him. "Do you blame me?"

"And everytime I said something about New Mexico, she thought—"

"Yes."

"But now Walter says that isn't what he said?"

"Right."

"But Tillie doesn't believe him?"

"I don't know. I think she's wavering."

Rafferty stared straight ahead, thunderstruck. "She really thinks I'm an E.T.?"

"She *wants* to," Brandy said carefully. "Aunt Tillie has this thing about science fiction stuff." She laughed softly, resting her hand on his chest. "Be grateful they didn't put you all behind bars tonight. She told me once that you could melt iron with your eyes if you wanted to. She would have had you trying it, just to satisfy her curiosity."

Rafferty groaned. "And how am I going to know what she decides? Or will I ever know?"

Brandy thought about it. "I think you will. Soon. If she calls you anything but Archer, I imagine it means you're off the hook, that she's finally given up her dream."

"Well, hell. And if she *does* call me that stupid name for the rest of my life?"

"She'll be in hog heaven," Brandy said cheerfully, turning to face him. "She'll watch you like a hawk, she'll twist everything you say, she'll always try to get through to you telepathically, and when we have children, God only knows how she'll act."

When he closed his eyes and groaned again, Brandy touched her lips to his chin. "Rafferty," she whispered, "are you really going to be around the rest of my life?"

His arms tightened and he lifted her until she was sprawled on top of him. Cupping her head with his large hand, he drew her closer. Closer. Until he felt her warm breath on his lips. Until the telephone rang.

Swearing, he untangled his fingers from her hair and reached for the receiver. "Yeah?" he snarled.

"Archer?" Tillie said cautiously.

Brandy wiggled to get more comfortable. When she was satisfied, she stacked her hands on his chest, rested her chin on them and watched him curiously. He looked up into the most beautiful eyes in the world and knew that whatever it took to keep her there in his arms, whatever price he had to pay, it would be worth it.

"Yes," he said decisively, "this is Archer."

His first reward was Brandy's face. A smile that rivaled the brightest sunlight touched her lips, her eyes. She nudged the receiver away from his chin and touched her lips to his. "I love you," she whispered against his mouth.

"Archer," Tillie said earnestly, "you should think about this. *Soon.* There is a nice little chapel in Las Vegas called the Bide a Wee. Or is it the Kirk in the Dell? Or maybe the—"

"Whatever it is," he promised gently, "we'll find it. I'll marry her, Tillie. First thing in the morning."

MORE ABOUT
THE SAGITTARIUS MAN

by Lydia Lee

The first thing you'd better know right off the bat before tangling with a Sagittarian man is that if you've got thin skin, you'd do better with a Pisces, because this man has one big flaw. What, only one? He is about as frank as they come. Opening his mouth and sticking his foot in it is an everyday event. Oh, but understand, he wouldn't hurt your feelings for the world. It's just that the words pop off his tongue with a life of their own, and like as not, they have an uncanny habit of hitting their mark. Perhaps it's because his symbol is the centaur, half archer-half horse, and you know what archers do: they draw their bows back, aim the quill, and zing, hit the bull's-eye. So, what's a gal to do? The best advice is to work on developing thick skin, but in the meantime realize that your Jupiter-ruled man means no harm.

We all know that no one's perfect, and as flaws go, a Sagittarian's imperfections are pretty easy to take. In fact, of all the signs, he's probably the most fun.

Sagittarians invented fun—add comedy, slapstick, circuses and general buffoonery. The good news is that their bon vivance is contagious. These guys are so optimistic that it almost borders on naivete. They are the life of the party; almost everyone likes a Sag, even after he's inadvertently insulted someone! Usually his words were intended as a compliment that sort of backfired. Now mind you, since this chap is having such a fine time rollicking through life he might be just a teensy bit antsy about settling down. Don't Fence Me In might well be his motto.

So, if you are enamored by a handsome Archer, give him lots of pasture, lots of rope, and never question his honesty. Believe me, he's honest! If he *were* seeing another woman you'd probably be the first to know. And if he is dangling after several prospects, don't sit home and mope. Chances are he'll come around once he sees what an independent and resourceful woman you are. Then when you are once again a duo, give the man so much freedom he won't know what to do with it! He might just find a cozy way to spend the time—with you.

Whatever the two of you do together, it will smack of stardust. You see, there's just something lucky about all Sagittarians. Undoubtedly beneficent Jupiter kissed them when they came into the world, gave them a silver spoon, and made them lucky in cards and love. Maybe it was to make up for their abysmal lack of tact and the way they blunder into things. But of all the signs, only a Sag can turn your tears to laughter in the blinking of an eye. It's his special brand of magic, and when those dark clouds rumble on your horizon, he'll show you their silver linings as you trip the light fantastic with him! Lucky you!

If you're interested in this outgoing, fun-loving fire sign, *and* you're prepared to keep up with him as he jaunts through life, a good place to find one is as close as your local travel agent—Sagittarians love traveling. Frequently they're associated with books: publishing, editing, writing or agenting. They make fantastic teachers and philosophers and explorers. He might even turn up in the guise of your friendly lawyer! However you meet your Sagittarian man, there's one thing for sure, your life together will be fresh and exciting. And although he might stumble a bit over the hearts and flowers, his love for you will be as exhilarating as an ocean breeze. And, as for all that luck that mighty Jupiter's going to rain down on the two of you...I'll leave that part up to your imagination.

* * * * *

FAMOUS SAGITTARIAN MEN

Kirk Douglas
Douglas Fairbanks, Jr.
Harpo Marx
George Segal
Charles Schultz

This is the season of giving, and Silhouette proudly offers you its sixth annual Christmas collection.

SILHOUETTE

Christmas Stories

1991

Experience the joys of a holiday romance and treasure these heartwarming stories by four award-winning Silhouette authors:

Phyllis Halldorson—"A Memorable Noel"
Peggy Webb—"I Heard the Rabbits Singing"
Naomi Horton—"Dreaming of Angels"
Heather Graham Pozzessere—"The Christmas Bride"

Discover this yuletide celebration—sit back and enjoy Silhouette's Christmas gift of love.

Silhouette Romance

LONG, TALL TEXANS

DONAVAN
Diana Palmer

Diana Palmer's bestselling LONG, TALL TEXANS series continues with DONAVAN....

From the moment elegant Fay York walked into the bar on the wrong side of town, rugged Texan Donavan Langley knew she was trouble. But the lovely young innocent awoke a tenderness in him that he'd never known...and a desire to make her a proposal she couldn't refuse....

Don't miss DONAVAN by Diana Palmer, the ninth book in her LONG, TALL TEXANS series. Coming in January...only from Silhouette Romance.

LTT192

WRITTEN IN THE STARS

WHEN A
CAPRICORN MAN
MEETS A
GEMINI WOMAN...

Wealthy dairy farmer Adam Challow's
no-nonsense approach to life wavered when
he met the enticing Gemini beauty, Donna
Calvert. The normally steadfast Capricorn
didn't want to trust his feelings, but Donna
was simply irresistible! Joan Smith's
FOR RICHER, FOR POORER is coming
this January from Silhouette Romance.
After all, it's WRITTEN IN THE STARS!

Available in January at your favorite retail outlet, or order your copy now by sending your
name, address, zip or postal code, along with a check or money order for $2.59 (please do
not send cash), plus 75¢ postage and handling ($1.00 in Canada), payable to Silhouette Reader
Service to:

In the U.S.

3010 Walden Ave.
P.O. Box 1396
Buffalo, NY 14269-1396

In Canada

P.O. Box 609
Fort Erie, Ontario
L2A 5X3

Please specify book title with your order.
Canadian residents add applicable federal and provincial taxes.

SR19